PRIDE OF THE COURTNEYS

When Louella Lloyd arrives at Courtney Hall, she is greeted by Lady Courtney with undisguised hostility, Sir Hugh with pained bewilderment and Georgiana with pleasure. But perhaps the most disturbing personality at the Hall is Bassett Courtney. Louella soon realizes that Lady Courtney's hatred for her springs from the closely-guarded secret surrounding her mother's connection with the Courtney family some years before Louella's birth. Only the friendship of Georgiana and Charles Corby sustain Louella when, suspected of theft, she becomes a prisoner of her fear of Bassett, Master of Courtney.

PRIDE OF THE COURTNEYS

Pride Of
The Courtneys

by
Margaret Dickinson

Magna Large Print Books
Long Preston, North Yorkshire,
England.

British Library Cataloguing in Publication Data.

Dickinson, Margaret
 Pride of the Courtneys.

 A catalogue record for this book is
 available from the British Library

 ISBN 0-7505-0786-1

First published in Great Britain by Robert Hale Ltd., 1968

Copyright © 1968 by Margaret Dickinson

Published in Large Print 1997 by arrangement with Darley
Anderson.

Magna Large Print is an imprint of
Library Magna Books Ltd.
Printed and bound in Great Britain by
T.J. International Ltd., Cornwall, PL28 8RW.

CHAPTER ONE

The news was broken to me in a gentle manner, I had to admit, but it was an unexpected shock.

'Louella, my dear, Lady Maria and I are going to be married,' Uncle James cleared his throat self-consciously and strode stiffly up and down the room, whilst I stood waiting, my eyes following his every movement.

'And I'm emigrating—to Canada.'

As he said the final disastrous words, he stood with his back to me, gazing out of the long window on to the smooth lawn, not daring to meet my eyes.

Motionless for several moments, I was about to ask if I was to go with them, but something held back the words. As he spoke again I was glad I had remained silent.

'I have arranged for you to go and live with my brother, Sir Hugh Courtney and his family, at Courtney Hall.'

Uncle James turned from the window

and as he came towards me I saw the anxiety in his eyes. He is trying not to hurt me, I thought.

'You'll be happy, Louella,' he was saying, taking my cold hands in his, 'they have a daughter about your age, Georgiana, you'll like her. And, of course Hugh—well, he's like me.'

It was a cruel and swift blow. I had no idea that anything like this was imminent. For four years, since Aunt Virginia had died, Uncle James and I had lived happily enough together. Why did he have to change all that? Why did he have to move so very far away, to another world almost? Lady Maria had been a constant visitor to the house for several months, but I had looked upon her visits as those of a friend only. I had been mistaken. Uncle James was to marry this handsome widow and return with her to her native country.

'You see, child,' Uncle James turned away and continued his restless pacing. He twisted his moustache, a trait so dear and familiar to me when he had something troubling him.

'You see, now you're getting older, people may start talking about you living

8

here with me. Oh, I know we have the servants,' he waved his hand in the air, 'but it's not the same as when—as when Virginia was alive.'

His gaze rested upon her portrait above the fireplace.

'You wouldn't understand, child,' he murmured, seeming to speak more to the life-like painting than to me. 'A Courtney and a Lloyd under one roof...'

Uncle James did not finish his sentence, but shook himself from the line of thought which I did not understand.

'Believe me, Louella my dear, it is for the best. Indeed it is.'

I had not spoken—I could not, the tears were too near. I ran from the room and up the stairs to my bedroom where I stayed until my emotions calmed. I was not one to cry. I despised weeping, fainting women. So, although my heart was breaking, the tears remained unshed.

Later, the maid helped me to pack. It seemed Uncle James had avoided telling me until the last possible moment because he felt so badly about it. I was to leave the next morning.

The day was warm and bright on the morrow, seeming to taunt me in my unhappiness. As I bade Uncle James good-bye I was calm, but the leaden weight of misery pressed down upon me, a weight which was not to be lifted completely for a long, long time.

'Louella, try not to think too badly of me. I would have it different if it were possible.'

'I will do as you say, Uncle James. But I shall miss you so. You're the only father I have ever known.'

For a moment, his face crumpled and I thought I should see something I had never seen before, a man weep. But tears are for women, or so I had always been told, and with a masterly control, Uncle James regained his composure.

'And you are the only daughter I have ever known.'

His hands gripped my shoulders and he clasped me to him for a moment. 'God be with you, my child.'

He released me suddenly and hurried away.

It was not my nature to run after him, to beg to be taken to Canada for I realised that even in a marriage between two mature persons, a third dependant was an unwanted burden.

What Uncle James had commanded, I must obey.

I climbed into the carriage and as we rattled down the drive, I looked back at the old house which I called home. It was not impressive as a building, but it was spacious and comfortable with beautiful grounds. Above all, it was a happy house, something which, in the following months, though I did not know it then, I was to appreciate as something rare and valuable.

Courtney Hall, as I remembered from occasional visits, was an awe-inspiring, palatial building set on a hillside in its own parkland, with a river and lake at its feet. The interior of the Hall was a maze of immense rooms, long passages and innumerable stairways.

Sir Hugh Courtney, Uncle James' elder brother, had inherited the major part of the land belonging to Sir James Courtney, their father. Sir Hugh, however, from the little I knew of him, was a mild, gentle man with no head for business or the running of the vast estate. The role of squire, which had been handed to him from his father, was more befitting his son, Bassett.

Bassett Courtney was the one member

of the family I had never met. Always, on previous visits I had paid to Courtney Hall, he had been away on business.

Lady Emily Courtney I remembered as a thin, tight-lipped woman, who obviously disapproved of Aunt Virginia, my mother's sister, and me, for some reason I knew not why.

It was four years since I had seen any of them when Sir Hugh and Lady Emily had attended Aunt Virginia's funeral. Georgiana would be twenty now as we were much the same age.

The journey was a long one to Courtney Hall, set on the Yorkshire moors and all the longer because I was so miserable and desolate.

The brilliantly sunlit countryside through which we travelled held none of the usual pleasure for me. The green fields and trees just bursting into leaf enveloped in peace and beauty, a sight which so often made me thankful to be alive, now only seemed to mock and emphasise my unhappiness.

At last, the carriage swept down the hill into Courtney Valley and up the opposite hillside to Courtney Hall standing guard over its dominions. The building formed a square with a courtyard in the centre, as I

The whole effect was one of richness and luxury. The Courtneys of Courtney Hall appeared to live in a far grander style than did Uncle James. But then, I reminded myself, Sir Hugh Courtney was the elder son, and this was the family inheritance, improved upon now, no doubt, by the famous young Bassett.

The butler returned and bade me follow him. I was shown into a large drawing-room. Seated on a brocade-covered chaise longue before a crackling log fire was Lady Emily Courtney.

She was as I remembered her, a straight-backed woman, rather angular because of her thinness; her grey hair piled high above a discontented face of sallow complexion, cold blue eyes and thin, almost non-existent, lips.

'Good afternoon, Miss Lloyd, you may come and sit down.'

She paused whilst I thanked her, walked forward and sat nervously in the chair opposite her. I had told myself not to allow her, or anyone else, to intimidate me, but meeting her hostile stare and noting the way she took in every detail of my appearance, it was difficult not to feel apprehension.

Obviously she was not pleased with what she saw. Finally, she sniffed her disapproval.

'Now you are to become one of the family at Courtney Hall, or so Sir Hugh and my son inform me—I feel it my duty to enlighten you as regards the family and your position. Remember one thing, Miss Lloyd, you are here on charity, by the goodwill and kindness of Sir Hugh certainly, but mainly by that of Bassett, my son,' and a note of pride crept into her tone. 'For Bassett Courtney is the master of Courtney Hall now—in every way,' and those hard eyes dared me to defy her words.

What a strange beginning, I thought. Clearly I was not welcomed here, at least, not by Lady Emily Courtney. I could not understand then why I had come at all. For I could imagine that a strong-minded woman such as Lady Emily could have exactly what she wanted—which was not my presence.

Somehow, someone had over-ruled her. I could not imagine it being the mild Sir Hugh. She had, I knew, dominated him all their married life—things were not likely to change now.

Lady Courtney pulled the bell-cord within easy reach from where she was sitting.

A neatly dressed maid entered.

'Show Miss Lloyd to her room, Mary.'

She turned back to me as I stood up.

'From now on, we shall all call you Louella. Naturally, you will address my husband and me as Sir Hugh and Lady Courtney.'

She paused, and I noticed the glint of pride again in her eyes.

'I think you should also address Bassett as Mr Courtney. After all, he is the master and squire of Courtney village although only thirty. Of course, you may call Georgiana by her Christian name.'

The last words were with the great condescension of bestowing a favour upon a servant.

'Very well, Lady Courtney, just as you wish,' I replied.

As I followed Mary, I realised that Lady Courtney was going to leave no doubt in my mind as to my position, and what I should and should not do. I resolved to keep my allotted place, but at the same time not to allow myself to be trampled upon. One can always preserve one's dignity and pride, I told myself, and this I would do, however overbearing the Courtney family became.

My room, however, held no note of being given to an unwanted waif. Indeed, its luxury overwhelmed me. I turned towards Mary and the question must have shown in my face, for she smiled kindly and said:

'It's all right, miss, this is the room the master said you were to have.'

I smiled and thought how like his brother Sir Hugh must be, so kind and thoughtful that he had insisted upon a beautiful room like this for me.

'Shall I help you unpack, miss?' the girl asked.

'Why yes, thank you. It would be a help.'

I liked Mary. She was a friendly girl. Though, no doubt, treated strictly as a servant by the Courtney family, I could not think of her as anything but a girl of my own age, and one who may be the only friend I would find here. Uncle James and Aunt Virginia had had servants, but they were so much like part of the family, that I should never treat any maid otherwise.

Mary, probably sensing I felt like this, chattered to me in a friendly manner telling me about the Courtney family.

'Miss Georgiana, she's a sweet person—you'll like her, miss. Not like madam, she's hard. The master's a bit like Lady Courtney, he's very stern, but I think he's kinder than her.'

'I always thought Sir Hugh was very gentle,' I put in.

'Oh yes, miss, Sir Hugh is. But I'm talking about the master, Mr Bassett.'

I stood up from bending over my trunk.

'Mr Bassett,' I exclaimed, 'the master. Do you mean *he* said I was to have this room? I thought you meant Sir Hugh Courtney.'

'Oh no, Sir Hugh's too wrapped up in his books to know what's going on.' She giggled mischievously.

'He probably won't notice you're here for a couple of weeks. He's kind and gentle, like you said, but he lives in a world of his own, miss. Now, Mr Bassett, he's the master of Courtney Hall and Courtney village, just like Lady Courtney told you down there. He's a very severe man, but a real gentleman. All the village folk worship him, miss.'

'Oh,' was all I could reply, for at that moment the door burst open and a beautiful girl whirled in. She was dark haired with olive skin and blue, blue eyes. I had never seen such a lovely, vivacious girl.

'Hello,' she smiled, dimpling prettily, 'you're Louella, aren't you?'

She came forward and took my hands in hers.

'I'm Georgiana Courtney. I'm so glad you've come—I do hope we shall be friends.'

For the first time since Uncle James had broken the news to me, my smile was genuinely warm.

'I'm sure we shall be, thank you for your welcome.'

'You're very pretty,' she remarked candidly as she looked me up and down.

'Why, thank you. And you're beautiful.'

'Oh nonsense,' she laughed, but the slight tinge of colour in her cheeks showed she was gratified.

'Come along, I'll show you the house,' and as she slipped her arm through mine and urged me towards the door, she spoke to Mary.

'Finish her unpacking, Mary, there's a lamb.'

'Of course, miss,' Mary beamed. It was easy to see she doted on Georgiana.

As we passed through the long corridors peeping into the grand bedrooms, Georgiana chattered gaily about the house, the furniture or the family.

When we went down to the first floor in the front wing of the house and into the long portrait gallery, she began to relate the family history of each portrait.

'This is Grandmother Courtney. See, Bassett looks like her, or rather the male edition of her looks. I'm supposed to, too, but she's far more beautiful.'

'Nonsense,' I assured her, 'you're the image of her.'

And she was.

'She was a very dominant person, strong and purposeful, just like Bassett,' Georgiana continued, 'but she was very hard and bitter, so father says. Grandfather didn't make her very happy. It was an arranged marriage—history repeats itself.'

'How do you mean?'

'Why—mother and father, of course. But you know all about that.'

'No, I don't.'

Georgiana's expression altered immediately.

'Then I have said too much, Louella, please forget it. Come,' and she urged me towards the next picture.

'This is Grandfather Courtney. Like father and Uncle James, isn't he?'

Looking at the portrait, it was like seeing Uncle James again. A lump came to my throat.

'He is certainly like Uncle James,' I murmured.

'But he wasn't as nice as father and Uncle. They are pets, absent-minded, but very sweet. But this one...' Georgiana shook her head, 'He was a philanderer and a spendthrift. If it hadn't been for Grandmother Courtney, we shouldn't have any wealth at all. As it is, with Bassett being like her and taking over now, we're getting richer and richer and richer.'

And she danced gaily down the long gallery, clapping her hands.

'Oh how I do chatter on,' she laughed, and she ran back and threw her arms about me. 'But it is so lovely to have someone to talk to, a real sister at last.'

Her face sobered.

'Louella, promise me that whatever

anyone says to you or the way they treat you, try not to let it worry you. Promise?'

I could not understand what she meant, but I could see by the seriousness of her voice and by the look in her eyes that she was genuinely concerned about something.

'Of course, but why...?'

'Never mind, come we'll go and see father.'

And again her cheerful, vital self, she pulled me away from the gallery, through a maze of passages and rooms to a small study on the ground floor.

As I stepped inside the cluttered room a small, middle-aged man glanced briefly over his spectacles at us. The dog, lying at his feet, barked a welcome.

'Ah Georgiana. And who is your friend?'

'Now, father, you remember. This is Louella Lloyd, you knew she was coming to live with us.'

The startled look in Sir Hugh's eyes and the fleeting expression, almost of pain shocked me. But then he got up and ambled towards me beaming pleasantly.

'My dear child, how welcome you are. My, my, Louella Lloyd, eh?'

And he shook his head in wonderment. At what, I did not understand.

'You're very beautiful, my dear, just like your mother.'

'You knew my mother?' I asked, delighted to find someone who could perhaps tell me more about the mother I had never known.

'Oh—I—yes,' he cleared his throat and turned away, obviously not wanting to discuss it. At the same time, I felt Georgiana's gentle hand on my arm pull me towards the door. As we left the room, Sir Hugh still muttered.

'A long time ago—a very long time ago.'

His shoulders hunched, his hand dithering, he suddenly looked years older than a few moments ago.

'Come, Louella, we must go,' Georgiana whispered and then raised her voice, 'See you at dinner, father,' and closed the door behind us.

'Father rambles a little, take no notice,' she smiled.

'But he said he knew my mother,' I began, but Georgiana changed the subject, deliberately, it seemed.

'I think you have seen most of the house

now, except the gardens, of course. But I should go and make sure Mary has done your unpacking. Change for dinner and come down to the dining-room in about half an hour.'

And with that she left me to find my own way back upstairs.

As I reached the first landing, I heard the heavy front door open and someone stride into the hall. I peeped over the banister.

A tall, dark man stood in the hall, handing his riding crop and hat to the butler. The top of his thick, black hair shone, and as he moved I could see his skin was weatherbeaten to a deep tan. He was very tall, one of the tallest men I had ever seen, very broad and he looked very strong.

As if I had spoken to him he looked up suddenly and saw me.

Our eyes met and held.

But he did not smile. His face, not particularly handsome, though ruggedly masculine was stern.

'You are Louella Lloyd, I suppose,' his voice resounded through the hall.

'Yes,' was all I could reply.

This man disturbed me, and suddenly

I realised why. This was the man about whom I had heard so much. This was the Master of Courtney Hall.

Bassett Courtney had arrived home.

CHAPTER TWO

It seemed a long time that we stood merely staring at each other. He, tall and stern-looking, in the hall of his home. I, a frightened unwelcome creature, peeping down foolishly over the banister from the top of the wide, sweeping stairs.

His rich baritone voice rang again through the hall making me jump.

'Come down, Miss Lloyd, and introduce yourself.'

His tone was so commanding, so befitting the master of Courtney Hall, that I obeyed demurely.

Nervously I went down and not until I stood before him did he speak again, this time towering above me.

His critical eye swept me up and down, and still he did not smile.

'So you are Louella Lloyd?' He seemed

to speak to himself more than to me, but it would be impolite not to reply I supposed.

'Y—yes, how do you do, Mr Courtney,' and I tried to smile weakly.

'How do you do, Miss Lloyd,' his grin was strong and warm. 'Then you know who I am?'

And then, without warning like the sun breaking through on a storm-tossed world, Bassett Courtney smiled.

'Welcome to Courtney Hall, Louella, I do hope you will be happy here.'

Ordinary words, yes, but the way in which Bassett voiced them, the manner in which he held out his hand and clasped mine gently but warmly, held such sincerity that my sensed reeled.

'I shall call you Louella since you are now one of the family.'

'Yes, of course,' I could hardly stammer.

'And you must call me Bassett.'

'But,' I blurted out, 'Lady Courtney, your mother, said I should call you Mr Courtney.'

He frowned and his face regained its former seriousness.

'I say you are to call me Bassett, that clear? Now, I expect you have to dress for dinner,' he said, 'see you then.'

And with that he left me, his long strides taking him swiftly down the long hall and into the drawing-room.

How diverse were the welcomes I had received. Lady Courtney—cold and openly hostile. Georgiana—joyously, Sir Hugh—shocked and bewildered, and now Basset—with warmth. Which, I asked myself, was the least expected? It was difficult to decide.

I did not feel quite so apprehensive as before. Georgiana was most certainly a friend, and Bassett was not a man who would feign an act of welcome. Though I could not help but fear him, his eyes were the most honest eyes I had ever seen. He was a man to be admired, I thought, but not to be crossed.

I returned to my room and from my few clothes I chose a brown velvet gown, which I considered most suitable for my first appearance at the Courtney table—unassuming, yet not lacking in elegance.

Accustomed to dressing myself without the help of a personal maid, I was ready for dinner with ten minutes to spare. I had not, I realised, had time to inspect the view from my room. I crossed the room and stood before the long window.

Although I had been given a back room, the view far surpassed my wildest hopes.

Immediately below my window a smooth lawn sloped gently down towards an orchard still richly laden with pink and white blossom. Beyond this glimmered the lake in the evening sun, and again beyond this the soft outline of purple hills. Tranquillity reigned supreme. I would have been content to stay there until the light faded and as it was, I was still staring breathlessly at the scene when the dinner gong sounded.

Dinner proved to be worse than I had imagined. For to add to my nervousness at being confronted by all the Courtney family at once, I found there were two guests for dinner.

Dr Charles Corby and his sister, Evelyn, were newcomers to the district and Bassett Courtney, being the squire, had asked them to dine as a note of welcome to his village.

Dr Corby was a young man of fair complexion. His face was handsome with finely chiselled features, and his expression was one of keen alertness. His eyes held the compassion and knowledge of so many dedicated to his profession. His sister, a little older than he, I guessed, was a plain girl, whose main asset was her fine brown eyes. She seemed quiet and withdrawn, even sulky. Her dress was unbecoming, though of good material.

I wondered why any girl of her age should show such a positive lack of interest in her appearance, for although neat, the whole effect was of a dull personality.

Lady Courtney made the introductions.

'This, Miss Corby, Dr Corby, is Louella Lloyd. The poor child has had the misfortune to be left a penniless orphan. My husband's brother has cared for her for many years, and now, his duty no doubt long expired, he has sought happiness in re-marriage and subsequent emigration.'

Here, whilst my cheeks slowly flamed, Lady Courtney paused significantly.

'So my husband, and son, I might add, feel it their duty to give this girl a home until such time as we may find a husband willing to take her, poor as she is.'

I realised it was unreasonable and unjust, but these were the words which sparked off my fear and dislike of Bassett Courtney. His mother's words implied that I owed everything to him, that but for his condescension and generosity, I should have been flung out on to the streets to live the life of many a ragged, orphaned urchin.

My acute embarrassment was somewhat lessened when Dr Corby smiled kindly, squeezed my hand a little more than necessary in his handshake and said gallantly:

'I'm sure, with such beauty, Miss Lloyd should have no difficulty in securing a husband.'

The reactions of everyone in the room to this remark were varied. I saw Lady Courtney raise her eyebrows slightly. A startled gasp escaped Miss Corby's lips—no doubt she was not used to hearing such forwardness from her gentle brother. But what dismayed me the most was that when I glanced at Georgiana, her expression was a mixture of hurt and anger.

But as she caught my eyes, she quickly hid her feelings and smiled brightly, if not successfully.

'She's well enough, I suppose,' Lady Courtney's answer was grudging. 'No doubt my son will find a suitable husband for her amongst the smaller landowners in the village.'

'A husband for whom, mother?'

My heart lurched. No one had seen Bassett enter at that moment. I sighed inwardly. Now I had to suffer yet more shame before his arrogant eyes.

'For Louella, of course. The sooner she is married, the better, as far as I can see.'

Bassett frowned.

'I don't see that there is any reason to hurry the poor child into an unhappy marriage.' He smiled sardonically at his mother. 'She'll hardly eat us out of house and home, mother.'

'Well, I sincerely hope you're grateful to Mr Courtney,' said Lady Courtney, turning to me. 'There's proof of his generosity indeed.'

My temper, though dangerously frayed, I managed to control and I answered her quite calmly, and I hoped with the right degree of humility, though it was difficult to keep the sarcasm from my tone.

'I am deeply indebted to Mr Courtney and to all of you for your kindness.'

There was rather an awkward pause. I felt Bassett's eyes upon me, but as I dared not meet his gaze I could not read his expression.

The tense atmosphere was broken suddenly by the appearance of Sir Hugh Courtney.

'Dear me, late again. I'm very sorry, Emily—Bassett.'

'Don't apologise, father. We were not ready ourselves.'

I noticed the difference in Bassett's tone when speaking to his father. It was gentle and respectful and gave no indication to a stranger that son, and not father, now held the status of head of the family.

Even at dinner, Bassett and Sir Hugh were seated at either end of the long table, so that it would be difficult for the uninformed to know who presided over the family gathering.

The conversation throughout the meal was centred upon the guests, and as I was not drawn into it, I ate in silence, not venturing to speak without invitation.

The same occurred when the ladies withdrew to the drawing-room, whilst the gentlemen drank their port, though I was somewhat heartened when Georgiana squeezed my elbow as we passed down the hallway.

Later, when the gentlemen rejoined us, Dr Corby deliberately seated himself next to me, and began asking me questions about myself.

'We seem to have neglected you, Miss Lloyd. Come, tell me about yourself.'

For some inexplicable reason, I felt the room grow cold and tense once more as the others fell silent. Lady Courtney glanced at her husband who in turn had fixed his attention upon me. As I met his gaze, it was as if he were seeing me for the first time. The same startled look crossed his face as when he had first seen me in his study. He breathed quickly and painfully.

I was distressed. Undoubtedly, something about me disturbed him every time my presence was called to his attention.

Lady Courtney, angered by the situation, sought to relieve the tension.

'Miss Lloyd has had an uninteresting life, Dr Corby. I am sure nothing of her conversation would amuse you. Now come, you must have had many varied experiences by which we would be entertained.'

'On the contrary,' Dr Corby's voice was polite, but no doubt he felt somewhat slighted, though not by me for I had

had no chance of replying to his question. 'My sister and I lived a very secluded life as children and since adolescence I myself have been so engrossed in work and study that I have seen very little of the outside world. Evelyn, too, in nursing our parents through their last illness, has allowed her youth to slip by unenjoyed.'

Bassett smiled at Miss Corby.

'I cannot agree that Miss Corby's youth has slipped away. Surely, she is only just beginning to enjoy it.'

Evelyn Corby smiled calmly, but the smile did not reach her eyes.

'You are very gallant, Mr Courtney. I am not ashamed to admit to my age, nor wish to hide it, like many women. I am twenty-eight and unmarried, and, according to the fashion of the day, that is decidedly old and quite definitely past the marriageable age.'

Bassett laughed, and it was as if the sun filled the room, sweeping away all sign of the tension of the previous few moments, between Sir Hugh and myself.

'It is absurd, the idea of today that twenty-eight is old. Why, it is a wonderful age for a young woman. I am thirty and unmarried. Now that must be thought ancient. And by now I cannot, surely, even hope for matrimony.'

Bassett's rich laugh infected us all, and soon even Lady Courtney was smiling.

'My dear Bassett,' she said indulgently, 'how plain it is to see you do not understand the ways of the world. While I beg you to believe me, Miss Corby, that I imply no insult to yourself for I think you very noble in your sacrifice to your parents, yet I must agree that twenty-eight is a little too old to begin securing a husband. However, let me hasten to assure you that you do not look a day over twenty-three, and there are plenty of young women unmarried at twenty-three.'

'You are very kind, Lady Courtney, to reassure me. But to be quite honest, I am not really interested in marriage. I am happy to care for Charles and keep house for him. A busy doctor needs an efficient homemaker.'

'But what if your brother should marry, Miss Corby?' Lady Courtney enquired.

Miss Corby hesitated and I thought a look of pain crossed her face.

'I am trained as a governess, I should not hesitate to seek employment. I would not wish to be a burden upon Charles.' And as she spoke I felt her glance at me—no doubt thinking of the burden I had become upon the Courtneys.

'Now, Evelyn, there is no need for such morbid talk,' said Charles.

'Really, Charles,' Miss Corby seemed distressed now. 'I have said too much already. Please, let us change the subject.'

Her discomfort, however, was short-lived for as Dr Corby left my side to talk to Lady Courtney and Georgiana joined them, I saw Bassett seat himself beside Evelyn and engage her in conversation.

Sir Hugh busied himself with a book at the far end of the room, and I was once more left alone.

After a few moments I slipped quietly and unobserved from their company and went to my room.

I was pleased to escape. The morning's parting from Uncle James, the various welcomes at Courtney Hall and tensions at dinner and afterwards had left me exhausted.

Within half-an-hour, I was in bed and just before I fell asleep, my last thoughts were of Bassett Courtney.

This proud, arrogant man over-awed me. I knew, without good reason, I did not like him. In his presence I felt a foolish, blushing child. And yet, it was because of him that I was here, cared-for and comfortable in beautiful surroundings. I ought to be grateful to him, but somehow my heart ruled my head and I could not, would not, like Bassett Courtney, because my pride rebelled against my dependence upon him for my livelihood.

The next morning I awoke with none of the forebodings with which I had fallen asleep. The sun streamed in through the window as Mary drew back the heavy curtains.

'Morning, miss,' she chirped, as I lifted my head sleepily from the pillow and blinked ridiculously in the bright light.

'Breakfast is in half an hour, miss. You are to have it in the old school room with Miss Georgiana, just for this morning.'

'Oh,' I faltered, 'where is that?'

'Of course, you'll not be knowing your way about this great house.' She paused. 'I'll slip back in half an hour and take you there, miss.'

'Don't trouble, Mary, you'll probably be busy.'

'No trouble, miss,' she smiled and added, obviously pleased with herself,

38

'the master told me last night I was to look after you, miss, and see you had all you wanted.'

'The master?' I queried hesitantly, already fearing the obvious answer.

'Yes, miss, Mr Bassett,' Mary said proudly, as she opened the door to leave.

I sighed silently.

Yet again, he was doing what he could for me. Why, I asked myself, could I not like him? Every time he favoured me with his attention to my welfare, it made me feel more indebted to him—in a way which I did not want.

Once out of bed, I went quickly to the window. I drew breath sharply. The view seemed even more beautiful than yesterday. Fresh and sparkling in the morning, the world seemed untarnished and so peaceful, that tears sprang to my eyes.

I turned at last from the panoramic view and hastened to dress. I could hardly wait to walk into the view and become a part of it.

I breakfasted alone. Georgiana had overslept after a late night entertaining their guests.

As soon as I could, I put on my outdoor wrap and leaving the great house,

I stepped joyfully into the grounds. I followed the path round from the front door to the back of the house, over which my bedroom window looked, and thence to the orchard.

I found a small gate at the far side of the orchard opening onto a meadow. I followed the winding cattle tracks towards the river. The rich grass, dappled with bright buttercups, still sparkled with dew in the spring sunlight, and the hem of my skirt soon became quite wet. But I did not care, for I was where I loved being. Alone with the peaceful world of nature. A rabbit bounced from the long grass and tore ahead of me. A cow lazily raised its head as I passed by and gazed at me with sorrowful eyes, ceaseless in its rhythmic chewing.

My heart felt lighter here away from the house and its strange atmosphere. There was something odd, I reflected. Why had Georgiana broken off so abruptly when talking about arranged marriages? Why had she spoken so seriously to me asking me not to be upset by anything anyone said to me?

And why was Sir Hugh so strange and distressed when my presence was called to his particular attention?

I sighed. Was I the centre of some mystery? And then I shook myself and laughed. I was being vain and foolish in thinking that I had any effect on the Courtney household other than that a homeless waif, as Lady Courtney called me, was an inconvenience.

I reached the river. Enchanted, I sat down on the bank and contentedly watched the water flow by placidly.

I must have remained there day-dreaming for a long time. For when I eventually shook myself and realised I ought to return to the house, the sun was high and warm on my back.

There was no doubt, I told myself, as I returned unwillingly to the Hall, in the coming days and weeks my happiest moments would be like this morning, spent on my own, alone with nature's peace.

As I climbed the stairs to go to my room, I heard the study door open and Bassett appeared.

'Louella,' his deep voice rang through the hall.

I turned, startled.

'Come down a moment.' His tone gave no intimation of the reason for his command. I wondered what reproof awaited me.

I went down quickly and stood meekly before him, not daring to look into his eyes.

Suddenly he raised his hand and cupped his strong fingers under my chin and raised my face to look at him.

'Don't look so frightened, Louella. I only want to ask you to come riding with me. I should like to show you round the estate and the moors. I have some spare time this afternoon.'

He paused, and I was surprised to hear the eagerness in his voice.

'Be ready as soon after luncheon as you can. Wear something warm, the air is sharp today.'

There again was his concern for my well-being, but I merely stammered assent.

'Bassett,' the sharp voice rang above us.

We both looked up. Lady Courtney stood at the top of the stairs. She must have heard us, I thought wildly, been watching us. Can she never leave me alone?

'Don't forget your cousin Millicent is coming this afternoon to stay for a few days. You should be here to greet her, you know.'

'We shall be back in time for tea, mother. Millicent should not arrive before that time.'

And without another word, he disappeared into his study.

There was no such escape for me.

I waited nervously whilst Lady Courtney came slowly down the wide stairs, her steps soundless on the carpet. She stepped close to me and pushed her wrinkled, sour face near to mine.

'What are you trying to do, Louella Lloyd,' she hissed, 'break another Courtney household, just like your mother before you?'

And with that she moved towards the drawing-room, her wide skirts sweeping angrily across the floor.

My heart beat painfully. Never before in my life had I come face to face with such obvious hatred. I ran upstairs to my room, and as I looked in the mirror I saw my face was pale, my eyes dark and fearful. I sat down and tried to calm myself. But the mood of depression would not leave me. I kept seeing Lady Courtney's angry face and hearing those awful words.

'...break another Courtney household, just like your mother.'

Whatever did it mean? What had my mother to do with the Courtneys, apart from being Uncle James' sister-in-law?

I was almost afraid to go down for luncheon, but I must of course.

The whole family were there, but this time, no guests. Lady Courtney was still smarting from her angry outburst, but her anger was now coldly sarcastic, which she made plain by criticising my clothes.

'I can see, Louella, we shall have to acquire you some different gowns. That one lacks taste, to say the least.'

Immediately, I felt Bassett's eyes upon me. His face was expressionless and he made no comment, but I was sure his mother had succeeded in making me appear small in his eyes, which now I was convinced was her only desire.

I was pleased to escape immediately after the meal and because, for some reason I could not understand myself, I wanted nothing to prevent my afternoon with Bassett, I changed into my riding habit, left the house quickly and somehow found my way to the stables to wait for Bassett.

I did not have long to wait, and I watched him approach from a distance before he saw me.

He looked a worried man, and I felt sorry for him, for, although I feared him, to have the responsibility of a great estate like this on his young shoulders, it must indeed be very worrying at times.

When he saw me, he smiled, and as he reached me, he said:

'That's one outfit I don't think dear mama will have to change. It becomes you admirably, madam,' and he gave a mock bow of courtesy.

I blushed for I thought he was laughing at me, and automatically my chin went higher.

'I am perfectly satisfied with the contents of my wardrobe,' I replied stiffly, 'they have always sufficed, and I see no reason to waste money on me.'

Bassett's eyes grew stern and suddenly I was afraid. Had I said too much and angered him.

'It would not be a waste of money spent on you, Louella, I assure you.'

The compliment, if it was one, was lost by his angry tone, and again I was annoyed that he should be considering providing my clothing, but I held my tongue—already I had spoilt what could have been a pleasant afternoon.

But no, suddenly Bassett smiled, took me by the arm and led me towards the stables.

'Come, Louella, let us not argue on such a beautiful afternoon. Forget our differences and let's enjoy ourselves.'

I was eager to do so and smiled warmly, the incident forgotten—for the moment.

We cantered steadily over the moors, Bassett matching his pace to mine, being slower than his usual I imagined.

'We'll let the horses rest at the stream.' His words came bouncing over the breeze to me. I merely nodded, I had not the strength of voice to reply.

We reined in and Bassett dismounted, and came to lift me down. I slid from the saddle into his arms.

For a brief moment he held me and as I looked up into his frowning face, I was at a loss to understand his expression. One of mingled anger and sorrow, was it? I could not be sure.

He released me and turned away.

'Come Louella, we'll walk to the rise whilst the horses drink.'

46

Meekly, I followed Bassett's long strides and soon we stood, breathless, at the top of the hill, gazing on the countryside around us.

Green fields patterned with hedges and copses rolled away to the blue hills in the far distance. The sun sparkled on the rich grass and the water of the stream, which widened into the river and then the lake before Courtney Hall, rippled and sang happily.

A sigh of sheer happiness and contentment escaped my lips. It was not often I felt so completely at ease or happy with the world.

The silence between us deepened, but it was not an uncomfortable one, although we hardly knew each other. How little I knew of this man, I thought. I believed I knew or understood the other inmates of the house, even though I had known them such a short time. But of this man, all I knew had been gained from other people's voiced opinions of him.

We returned from the hillside and remounted. Downhill we rode over the fields, through wooded slopes, down to the river.

The water lazily rolled its way from

the hills above us down to Courtney village and away to the sea. It seemed peaceful and harmless enough so that I was surprised and almost disbelieving when Bassett said:

'I am afraid we are expecting trouble next winter.' His eyes wrinkled against the sun as he scanned the village and fields beneath us in the valley.

'Trouble? What sort of trouble?' I asked.

Somehow, out here, just the two of us, I did not feel so afraid of him. My dislike of Bassett seemed to diminish in the warm sunlight.

'The old men of the village say there will be heavy snowfalls and a danger of the river flooding when it melts.'

'The poor villagers!' I cried.

Bassett glanced at me swiftly. I could not understand the fleeting expression of surprise and pleasure on his face. But it was gone in a moment as he said:

'Not that I believe in all this forecasting the weather, but these old men, living all their lives in the country, have an uncanny knack of being able to foretell such disasters. I've known it before.'

Bassett paused as our horses forded a narrow stream. He guided my horse up

48

the steep slope at the other side.

'Fifteen years ago, old Hawkins, he's dead now, said there would be a drought. Most people in the village, the young men that is, laughed at him and took no heed. He came to the Hall one day and pleaded with my father to take all possible precautions against the drought, to store as much water as he could. My father, always ready to listen to advice, did what Hawkins said.'

Bassett paused.

'What happened?' I looked towards him impatiently.

'The drought came. The villagers lost their crops. The Courtneys did not. They made even more money to add to the ever-increasing pile.'

'You sound bitter. Don't you like to be wealthy, Bassett?'

'It does not bring happiness, little Louella,' Bassett said gently. 'I would give all my Courtney wealth if I could be sure I would find happiness.'

I was astonished that Bassett, a man who seemed above all emotion, should open his heart to me. He must, I thought, feel the atmosphere of tension at Courtney Hall as I do. I did not mention his own family, however. I thought it wiser not to do so.

'Uncle James and Aunt Virginia were always poor, but very happy.'

The familiar lump rose to my throat as I thought of the happy days I had known with them, and the ache of loneliness swept over me.

'Uncle James was wise, he put happiness before wealth. My father was weak-willed. He would have been happy if...'

But Bassett said no more, for at that moment, a carriage came into view on the road a short distance from us.

'Millicent Bassett,' he murmured. 'Wait here, Louella. I had better greet her.'

And he cantered away to where the carriage was already slowing down.

I was disappointed he had been interrupted. Perhaps what he had been going to say would have helped solve this mystery which seemed to surround the Courtneys and me.

I watched as Bassett stopped before the carriage. The face of a young woman appeared at the window. Although I was too far away to see clearly, I had the impression that Millicent Bassett was far from plain, and was dressed grandly. I saw Bassett take the slim gloved hand through the window and caught the sound of gay, girlish laughter as Millicent greeted her cousin.

Millicent looked up, and over the sunlit grass our eyes met. Bassett turned and beckoned me.

With a sinking heart, I turned my horse towards them. I had not been mistaken. Millicent was very attractive and to me her appearance was far superior to my own.

I smiled uncertainly as Millicent's eyes took in every detail of my appearance. Immediately, I felt dishevelled. But Millicent's voice belied her looks, it was the whining voice of a discontented, spoilt child.

'How do you do, Miss Lloyd? I am pleased to make your acquaintance. I believe the Courtneys have been kind enough to give you a home—for the moment.'

I saw the look of veiled dislike in Millicent's cold, blue eyes.

She hates me, I thought, and we have only just met.

Then my pride came to my rescue, and a spark of anger made me reply coldly.

'Yes, Miss Bassett. I shall never be able

to repay them for their kindness. I trust you have had a good journey?'

I saw the flash of anger in Millicent's eyes. She had wanted me to cringe and stammer. I had won the first point in what was evidently going to be a battle.

'Thank you, Miss Lloyd, I have.'

'We must finish our ride, Louella. We'll see you later, Millicent.'

Millicent turned her eyes towards Bassett and a flirtatious smile lit her face.

'*Au revoir*, Bassett,' and playfully she kissed her hand to him.

The carriage drew away and Bassett and I turned our horses towards the river bank again.

But the afternoon was spoilt for me. I could not recapture the feeling of companionship with Bassett which I had felt growing between us before Millicent had arrived. It was as if the wall of misunderstanding was built up between us again.

And I did not realise then that these few hours in Bassett's company were to be the closest to happiness that I was to feel for several months.

When we returned, we entered the house together. Lady Courtney met us and though no doubt she was displeased to see us together, she had more urgent matters on her mind.

I left them and began to climb the stairs but I could not help overhearing their conversation.

'Mrs Smith has been to the Hall this afternoon. She is most distressed because you have dismissed her son from your employ. May I be permitted to ask why, Bassett?'

'Certainly, mother. The boy was found to be a petty thief. You know I cannot abide dishonesty in any form. And there's an end to it.'

'But the boy is only fourteen and it was only a few eggs he took, Bassett. Mrs Smith begged for a second chance for him.'

'The younger he learns right from wrong the better. I shall not ruin his chances of employment elsewhere, but he is dismissed from Courtney estate.'

And with that he left his mother.

In those few moments, I discovered two things. Firstly, there was no mercy in Bassett Courtney. Secondly, there was thought for others in Lady Courtney—except for me.

CHAPTER THREE

The weeks passed at Courtney Hall, Millicent's stay of three or four days lengthened into weeks and months. Lady Courtney had obviously found a staunch ally in Millicent in her dislike of me. They lost no opportunity of reminding me of my position, nor of trying to goad me into losing my temper.

Being red-haired with a fiery temper, I found the natural retorts hard to restrain and often I went to bed at night, feeling physically and mentally exhausted with battling against my inner emotions, whilst trying to assume an uncaring expression.

I avoided their company as much as possible, and when I was not with Georgiana, I preferred my own company to that of Lady Courtney or Millicent. I hardly saw Sir Hugh and Bassett was occupied a great deal with the running of the estate. His spare time was taken up by Millicent as often as she and Lady Courtney could contrive it. For it was not only Lady Courtney's dearest wish that Bassett should marry Millicent, her brother's daughter, but also the only thing for which Millicent lived and designed.

Hence her prolonged stay at Courtney Hall. Bassett was not an easy prey and Millicent's marriage contrivances would be long and arduous. I was amused by Millicent's artless flirtations with Bassett.

'She positively throws herself at him,' as Georgiana remarked to me in disgust. 'I wonder he can stand it.'

Georgiana had no affection for Millicent, for the latter was indulgent and pleasant towards her merely because she was Bassett's sister and she knew that Bassett loved Georgiana dearly. This was another of her ways of currying favour with Bassett, befriending Georgiana.

But Miss Georgiana, strong-willed and fearless, would have none of Millicent's insincere attempts at friendliness.

Georgiana and I soon became the firmest of friends and I was to find her a great comfort and strength in the months ahead.

There was one and only one point on which we disagreed. She worshipped and idolised Bassett whereas I disliked him. But even this did not seriously impede our friendship. On my side I was only too happy to have such a strong ally and on her side she was confident that it was because I did not know Bassett that I hated him and that as soon as I did, I could not help loving him as she did.

Dr Corby and Evelyn were constant visitors to Courtney Hall. Evelyn, though pleasant enough towards the Courtney family, kept herself aloof, and always had about her an air of sadness.

Georgiana's romantic mind confided to me that she believed Miss Corby must have been disappointed in love.

'Really, Georgiana,' I admonished with mock severity, 'you think of nothing, but love and marriage.' Georgiana's black curls danced merrily.

'And what, dear Louella, do you consider is more interesting than discussing what is, after all, all we girls have to hope for?'

'Nonsense,' I retorted, 'the times are changing. Many girls earn their own living as governesses—or something,' I ended lamely.

'Yes, I agree,' she replied, 'but I have such a feather brain, I cannot remember the simplest lines of poetry, never mind Greek and Latin and arithmetic.'

She paused and I did not fail to notice the faint tinge of colour in her cheeks nor the dreamy expression in her eyes as she said,

'Dr Corby must be very, very clever.'

'Indeed, medicine is a hard profession, and one, I believe, in which the learning is never ended, for they are always making new discoveries.'

This conversation was taking place in a small summer-house overlooking the lake some two hundred yards from the house, one warm day early in June.

A boat appeared round a curve of the bank some twenty yards out upon the smooth water. Lazily, our conversation ceased and we watched the lithe figure of the oarsman as his firm, clean strokes cut the water and his craft skimmed along leaving ripple upon ripple ever-widening until they lapped softly against the bank.

Hearing Georgiana draw a swift breath, I glanced at her. There was no mistaking the pleasure in her expression and voice as she whispered.

'It's him, Louella, it's Dr Corby.'

And with that she jumped up, straightened her skirt and walked down the short sloping path to the edge of the lake.

She waited a moment until Dr Corby had seen her, and then she waved. Dr Corby skilfully turned his boat towards the bank and in minutes they had joined me in the summer-house.

I had observed their meeting from a distance, and though his greeting was formal, I did not fail to notice that his eyes rarely left her face, and that she was more radiantly beautiful in his presence.

'Good day, Miss Lloyd,' he said in greeting.

'Good day, Dr Corby,' I replied, and we smiled at each other.

I knew he was a friend, for often when he visited Courtney Hall, he would search me out and hold long conversations with me, which I was sure he did out of pity for my lonely existence.

We all sat down in the summer-house, with Dr Corby between us.

'It is time you called us by our Christian names, Dr Corby,' Georgiana said.

'Thank you. Nothing would give me greater pleasure, and please call me Charles. But will your mother or Sir Hugh be displeased?'

'Fie, and I don't care if they are,' she retorted, pouting prettily.

Georgiana made her own decision, Charles should know by now, I thought. Although she is only young, once she has made up her mind to something, nothing would change her.

And so we passed a pleasant afternoon in Charles Corby's company, but when we returned to the house and he sped away in his boat, I noticed Georgiana seemed subdued and quiet.

'Is anything wrong, Georgiana?' I asked, for she was never sulky or cross for long, it was not her nature.

Georgiana smiled immediately, but I knew it was an effort. 'Of course not, how could there be?' And she linked her arm with mine.

As we entered the hall, Bassett was emerging from his study. Georgiana ran to him at once and he swung her round playfully.

I watched them and thought how wonderful it must be to be loved by a brother like Bassett Courtney. I had not only missed the joy of having real parents to bring me up, I thought, I had missed also being part of a family.

'Bassett,' Georgiana was saying, 'I have been thinking for some time now, it is time

Louella was shown the Courtney dagger, is it not? And you are the one to show her. Will you?'

Bassett turned and smiled at me, his brown eyes kindly.

'Why, of course, if Louella is interested.'

'This is the first I have heard of it, but yes, I should like to see it.'

'We'll go this minute,' cried Georgiana and she dragged Bassett away by his arm. We all laughed and gaily Georgiana led the way to the portrait gallery which she had shown me on the day of my arrival.

We went past the portraits of the Courtney ancestors to a door half-way down one side of the long gallery hidden behind a blue velvet curtain.

Bassett lifted the curtain, opened the door and held it for us to pass into the room.

I gasped as I looked round. The room was filled with priceless silverware, clocks, china and jewellery. I had never seen such valuable articles nor so many all together.

'These are the Courtney riches in possessions, Louella,' Bassett explained. 'You will go a long way before you find a larger collection.'

But as he spoke there was no note of

pride in his voice as one might expect. He was merely making a statement. He led me to a large glass case at one side of the room. In it were two silver tankards, a gold watch, a silver bracelet, a diamond necklace and one of pearls, and other small articles. But all were overshadowed by a magnificent dagger lying on a black velvet cushion in the centre of the case. It was solid gold with three large rubies on its handle, and six smaller diamonds spaced out down the blade which finished in a wicked point, the sharpness a jewel itself.

'The Courtney dagger,' Bassett murmured, and this time his tone was full of pride. 'It is the only thing in this room which I care about, Louella.'

Gently, he unlocked the case and lifted the dagger out. All three of us stared at the beautiful but dangerous weapon.

'Shouldn't it be locked away somewhere safer than a glass case?' I queried, 'if it so very valuable.'

Bassett smiled.

'No one can get into Courtney Hall and as far as this without someone knowing, I am sure,' Bassett said frowning slightly. 'The only danger comes from those within Courtney Hall itself. But I think the servants are all honest and trustworthy.'

'Tell her the story about the dagger,' urged Georgiana.

'Many years ago, almost three hundred, one of our ancestors, Sir William Courtney, went to war for Queen Elizabeth. He won many battles and succeeded in gaining Her Majesty's particular notice. As a token of her gratitude for his bravery and loyalty to her and his country, she presented him with this dagger, saying that he should never let it go from the Courtney family, but that it should be passed down from generation to generation.

'Over the years, the superstition grew around the Courtney dagger that as long as it was in the possession of the Courtneys they would prosper and flourish. It did not,' Bassett's tone hardened slightly, 'promise happiness, but one cannot expect everything of it. However, this superstition grew strong amongst the Courtneys, especially when certain happenings seemed to strengthen the idea.

'A later Courtney, the first Sir William's great grandson, I think, was a philanderer and cared nothing for such superstitions. He landed himself heavily in debt and cared no more than to sell the dagger to help repay his debts.'

Bassett paused.

'He had reason to regret his hasty and unthinking action. He died a violent death by drowning. His son, realising the folly of his father's ways, worked hard, and although the Courtney estates were in jeopardy, he managed to make enough money to buy back the dagger. He was fortunate to be able to do so. But it happened that the man who had bought it was pleased to be rid of it again, for since he had bought it nothing but misfortune had befallen him.'

'He lost his son, again by drowning,' put in Georgiana, 'and being a landowner like the Courtneys, he lost all his crops in a drought, which nearly crippled him, and then the next year, as he had managed to plant more crops, he lost all those in a flood. So the poor man was ruined. Then the superstition really grew strong that if the Courtneys let the dagger go, misfortune will befall them, and whoever takes it from them, the same thing will happen to them—nothing will go right for them until the dagger is returned to the rightful owner, the Courtneys.'

'And what happened when the dagger

was returned to the Courtneys?' I asked.

'Everything began to go right,' said Georgiana, 'the Courtneys flourished, and the poor man who was ruined because he had bought it also prospered.'

'The same sort of thing almost happened more recently,' said Bassett. 'My grandfather, you have seen his portrait in the gallery, haven't you?'

I nodded.

'You mean the one like Sir High and Uncle James?'

'Yes, but he was not like them in character.'

'No, Georgiana told me,' I replied. 'But for your grandmother the Courtneys would not be where they are now.'

Bassett smiled, but without humour.

'In more ways than one, I fear. But to get back to the dagger. My grandfather, Sir James Courtney, worked hard in his youth on the Courtney estate and added considerably to its wealth. He made a brilliant marriage, as they say, meaning my grandmother, Lady Florence Cunningham, was an heiress. In his middle age, though, Sir James grew tired of hard work and went to London to "live" a little.

'A country gentleman born and bred was

no match for the smart set of London and foolish Sir James was soon relieved of his fortune. He sold much of the family wealth and land, including the dagger, before my grandmother found out. Fearing the worst would happen, and in fact distressing incidents did take place...'

Bassett paused momentarily in his tale, and I saw the look which passed between Georgiana and himself, and noticed Georgiana's slight shake of the head, as if to tell Bassett he was treading on dangerous ground, for he cleared his throat and hastened to finish his story.

'Grandmother used her own money to regain the lost fortune and set the Courtneys to rights, as far as she could. She again managed to recover the dagger from its purchaser, who once more was pleased to be rid of it.'

'Has it never been stolen?' I remarked, running my fingers idly along the shimmering stones.

'No, and I pity the thief who does, for he will surely regret it,' said Georgiana fiercely.

'Do you believe these superstitions, Bassett?' I asked.

'I don't know really, Louella,' he said

thoughtfully, as he replaced the dagger in its glass case. 'I am not a man who readily believes such fairy stories, but there does seem to be some uncanny power with this small dagger. Still, it is pleasant to think that whilst we have it, we cannot be cast into the streets to live as beggars.'

'I wish I had something to safeguard me in that way,' I could not stop the words, but immediately I wished I had.

'Now that is the most foolish remark I have ever heard you utter, Louella,' he said. 'You seem to have little faith in our desire to help you.'

My heart beat painfully. Bassett was really angry this time. There was nothing I could do but apologise.

'I'm sorry, I did not mean to be ungrateful, but at times I feel so dependent on you, it is uncomfortable, to say the least.'

'Then don't feel that way.'

And Bassett left the room quickly.

'Oh Louella,' moaned Georgiana, 'you have put your foot in it this time.'

I was distressed, and angry with myself. Although inwardly I had disliked Bassett, and still did, because I owed him so much, at the same time to voice such thoughts was ingratitude in the extreme, and I did not wish to show that.

We left the room of treasures and walking by the portraits of Bassett's grandparents, I looked at them with fresh interest. Grandmother Courtney sitting very erect, was stern and forbidding and so very like Bassett in her expression. But I could see from where Georgiana got her beauty. Although the picture had been painted when Lady Florence was old, there was no mistaking the fine features and proud bearing.

'There's another picture of her when she was younger,' said Georgiana, 'Look down here,' and tucked away at the end of the long gallery was a smaller painting of Lady Florence.

'Why, she looks a different person,' I exclaimed. It was as if Georgiana stared back at me from the canvas. Lady Florence had most certainly been a beautiful woman, but in this portrait she showed none of the hardness which was apparent in the later one.

'She was lovely in this one, wasn't she?' said Georgiana, 'I think her unhappy life made her bitter and cynical by the time the other one was painted.'

'How terrible,' I cried, 'that someone with such beauty should live an unhappy life.'

'It is the way of the world, Victoria,' a voice spoke sadly behind us. Georgiana and I spun round to see Sir Hugh Courtney in the doorway.

'Why, father,' welcomed Georgiana. 'Bassett and I have just been showing Louella the dagger and telling her about it.'

I noticed that she stressed my name. I could not understand why Sir Hugh had called me Victoria, my mother's name.

Sir Hugh came up to us and stood thoughtfully gazing at the portrait of his mother.

'She was very beautiful, Sir Hugh,' I said shyly.

'Yes, but she was very cruel, my dear.'

He turned to Georgiana and put his hand on her shoulder. She moved closer to him, for I knew she was very fond of her absent-minded father.

'Georgiana, my dearest child, you are the living image of your grandmother. But as you go through life, be sure you don't cause the same unhappiness to your family as she did. Beauty is not everything, happiness should come first.' And his voice broke painfully. As if he could trust himself to say no more he left us swiftly.

What a strange afternoon.

As I went to my room, the events flooded through my mind. Georgiana's obvious attraction for Dr Corby would surely lead to a rift in the family if it became stronger and if Charles were to reciprocate. Bassett was obviously angry with me for my thoughtless remark in the 'treasure room' as I called it. And now Sir Hugh, firstly calling me Victoria and then displaying such emotion before his mother's portrait.

I sighed. Dear me, this was a household of mystery and emotion, I thought. Gone were the peaceful, uncomplicated days I had known with Uncle James and Aunt Virginia.

My fears regarding Georgiana's growing affection for Charles were soon justified. At any rate, to me.

Whenever his name was mentioned, her eyes sparkled and an attractive blush suffused her cheeks. And in his presence, she became more alive than ever, if that was possible for she was such an energetic person all the time.

But unfortunately Charles did not seem to return her affection to such a degree. Admittedly he was most attentive to her and whenever she was present, he could not prevent his eyes from straying to her lovely face continually. But then, what young man could resist her beauty?

But it was to me that he paid the greatest attention. He began to ask me to go for walks with him, and though this might have been considered improper, Lady Courtney readily agreed to me being allowed to go with him unchaperoned, for she was already beginning to look upon him as a possible husband for me.

But there were others who did not look upon this friendship with such glee. I was amused to see that I had at last pleased Lady Courtney on one point, but those who were displeased distressed me.

One, naturally, was Georgiana, and day by day she seemed to grow more reserved and distant with me. This, of course, upset me considerably for she was the greatest friend I had, and had I been in love with Charles, I should have been in two minds whether to reject his attentions because of Georgiana, so great was my affection for her.

But I knew I was not, and never would be, in love with Charles. If anything, he was the brother I had always wanted, and indeed a dear friend, but I could never entertain the idea of him being my husband.

I wondered how I could tell Georgiana this, but she had never confided her feelings for Charles to me, and it was all surmise on my part that this was the cause of her unhappiness. But it was obvious that each day she grew more miserable.

My friendship continued to grow with Charles and was frowned upon by his sister, Evelyn. She, I concluded, had given her life in service, firstly to her parents, and now to her young brother. I learnt, from Charles, that she had been the cause of him becoming a doctor in the first place. Though he was loyal to his sister, and I believed he was very fond of her, Charles felt somewhat restricted in the same way I did with the Courtneys, because he owed her a debt of gratitude.

'At the time our parents died,' Charles told me one day as we strolled companionably over the moors, 'Evelyn was twenty and I seventeen, and studying hard at school. Evelyn was sufficiently educated to be a governess, and rather than let me work to keep us both, she took a post so that I could continue my studies.'

We sat down beneath a tree.

'Our parents left us poor, and needless to say, by the time the funerals were paid for, they died within three days of each other, there was no money left.'

'How dreadful for you to lose them so close together,' I murmured.

Charles shrugged.

'Neither Evelyn nor I felt much love for them. My mother was a weak, bad-tempered creature. I hate to speak ill of the dead, Louella, but believe me it is the truth. And my father was a blustering drunkard most of the time. Not the most congenial surroundings for two sensitive children.'

I thought about Evelyn Corby. No doubt she inherited her mother's sulkiness, but she was by no means weak. I was beginning to see that she doted on her brother and had him exactly where she wanted him—in her power because he was grateful for the sacrifice she had made for him.

Charles continued.

'Evelyn worked so that I might study. Because my parents had suffered considerably in their last months, Evelyn decided that I should become a doctor. The idea appealed to me, though I was a little doubtful of my capabilities. However, I progressed well and my tutors were pleased, and here I am now in my first practice, a fully-fledged doctor.' And he added with sincerity, 'I hope I succeed as a doctor, Louella.'

I knew he needed reassurance.

'Of course you will. Why people in the village already speak highly of you, and you have only been here a short time. Mrs Walters is an ardent follower of yours since you eased her little boy's bronchitis so quickly. And, believe me, she holds considerable sway in the village amongst the ladies, so Mary tells me.'

'You're very kind, Louella, to encourage me so. I have met with opposition since I arrived here, but mostly from the older folk who don't trust my youth. I must admit, though, there's not been as much distrust as I expected.'

'Kindness, no, Charles, I'm being truthful.'

'I think probably the Courtneys' friendliness is an undoubted asset.'

We fell silent. I was thinking of Georgiana and I wondered if Charles was too.

Strangely enough, when we returned to the house, it was Georgiana who met us. A very distressed Georgiana. In her unhappiness she had forgiven her anger with me over Charles for she flung herself into my arms, her eyes red with weeping.

'Louella, the most dreadful thing, you must help me. I won't do it, I can't.'

I glanced at Charles and was heartened to see his face was contorted with distress at Georgiana's misery. Perhaps he does care for her, I thought. But these thoughts were cut short, for I had to attend to Georgiana's immediate problem.

'My dearest, what is it? Tell us.'

'Not here. I can't tell you here,' she whispered, and glanced over her shoulder fearfully.

'Come quickly to the summer house, then.'

And together, the three of us hurried down to the summer house near the lake.

When we had settled down with Georgiana between us, I made her tell us the whole story from the beginning, promising we would do all we could, whatever it was.

Although her eyes filled with tears, she began bravely.

'The first I knew about it was this afternoon, just after you had gone out. Mother called me down to the drawing-room. Father was with her, and Millicent. Mother said she had something to tell me of the utmost importance and that I must tell no one for the moment, until further plans had been made, but she thought it only fair to tell me now,' Georgiana gulped painfully.

'She said that arrangements were under way for a marriage between—between Cedric Rothbone—and—and—me.'

From her tone of voice, the idea was repulsive to her, without the fact that she loved Charles, as I believed she did.

'What?' Charles exclaimed. 'An arranged marriage with someone you hardly know. Do you know him, Georgiana?'

'No, I've never heard of him before today. Evidently, he is the son of Lord Rothbone, who lives on a grand estate, almost the size of ours about fifty miles away. Mother's brother, Major Phillip

Bassett, you know, Louella, Millicent's father, is well acquainted with Lord Rothbone. He was evidently interested in an alliance between his son, Cedric, and Millicent. But—but, Uncle Phillip and mother have always been set on Millicent and Bassett marrying, so that Uncle Phillip suggested me, to Lord Rothbone, instead of Millicent.'

And here she burst into fresh tears.

I patted her hand comfortingly, though I could not think what to say. She was too young to disobey her parents' wishes.

'Your only hope is Bassett. Surely he would not make you marry someone whom you did not love?'

'Bassett wasn't there, but mother says he is in full agreement, and to his marriage to Millicent. We are to have a double wedding in September,' she wailed.

'Did she say anything else?'

Georgiana hesitated and glanced at me.

'Well—yes—but I don't think...'

'Come, you must tell us everything,' Charles prompted gently.

'But it's about you,' she replied. 'And Louella.'

'About me?' he exclaimed.

'Me and—Louella?' he repeated stupidly.

'I fail to see where we fit in, do you, Louella?'

I did, but I shook my head.

'She says that there may be three weddings,' whispered Georgiana, and looked more dejected than ever.

'What?' Charles looked incredulous, then he laughed. 'Your mother seems to be arranging everyone very nicely,' he said, but with a note of sarcasm. Georgiana failed to catch that note, and no doubt presumed that he agreed with her mother.

'But the main problem is you,' said Charles briskly. 'You must see Bassett. Louella is right, I am sure he would not hasten you into an unhappy marriage. And if you have no success, then Louella or I must see him.'

'Would you? Perhaps it would do more good if you saw him, but—oh dear—I am not supposed to have told you. No, we'd better wait a while until it becomes public knowledge, then start objecting,' said Georgiana, now regaining her composure and her strength of mind.

'One thing is certain, I will not marry the odious man.'

We stayed a little longer until Georgiana had calmed herself more and though there were still traces of her tears when we returned to the house, she had recovered from her weeping.

Charles left us to go home and Georgiana and I went to her room to talk about the problem more.

I sat down opposite her and took her cold hands in mine.

'Now listen to me, Georgiana. We have been good friends and I hope we still are. You have been good to me since I first came here, and I am grateful. But recently, something has been wrong, you have grown colder towards me. Now why?'

She looked away out of the window and did not want to meet my eyes. But I was determined to hear it from her own lips that she loved Charles.

'I'm sorry, Louella, it is not your fault. Mother has been talking about you and Charles being married, and now, my marriage, oh dear...'

I did not want her to suspect that I thought I knew what was wrong, so I feigned ignorance and said,

'Perhaps you will fall in love with Cedric when you meet him. He may be a fine man.'

'How could I?' she cried angrily, 'when... when...'

'When what?'

'When I love someone else,' she ended in a rush.

'Who?' I persisted.

'I—I can't say.'

'Do I know him?'

This seemed to strike her as funny.

'I'll say you do, I mean...' But the damage was done.

'Well,' I said slowly, 'the only eligible male I know outside the family is Charles.'

And Georgiana's cheeks flamed.

'So it is Charles,' I said softly.

And she began to cry.

'I'm so sorry, Louella. I didn't want to tell you, but you can be persistent when you want to be. I know you love him and he loves you, so please don't tell him, will you? Please.'

'*I* love him, whatever are you talking about, Georgiana?'

I pretended shocked surprise, but this was the moment I had been waiting for, to tell her that I had no romantic love for Charles Corby.

'You—you do love him, don't you?'

'No, I don't and what is more, he

79

doesn't love me. We are the best of friends, I admit, but that is not love and marriage. Now get that idea out of your silly head, do you hear?'

I hoped I spoke sternly for I meant to do so. To a girl in love the world seems distorted, and she could see no reason why I did not love the man she loved so dearly.

'Louella,' her eyes were bright with happiness, 'you mean you are not going to marry Charles, but,' her face fell again, 'he probably wants to marry you.'

'Rubbish,' I said, 'why if he had any matrimonial intentions towards me, he has had plenty of opportunity to express them to me on our outings together.'

'I know. Oh, Louella, I am so happy, so relieved. I tried not to be jealous of you, but I was. And I loved you so at the same time, and Charles, I was so torn.'

'A beautiful creature like you being jealous of me,' I laughed. 'Why there's flattery for you.'

'You're beautiful yourself if you only think so, your auburn hair and green eyes. You are, Louella, else why do you think mother and Millicent fear you?'

'Fear me?'

'Yes, of course. Mother fears you because—because of the past, and Millicent because of Bassett.'

'The past? What happened, Georgiana, you must tell me?'

'No,' and her tone was firm, 'that I cannot tell you for it is not my secret. And one thing I do not do is break confidences. I'm sorry, I wish I could tell you because I think you ought to know. But there it is—I can't.'

'Very well,' I sighed, 'but I should dearly love to know. But Millicent, you say, how can she be afraid of me concerning Bassett?'

Georgiana looked at me strangely.

'If you haven't noticed Bassett's interest in you, you're the only one who hasn't. And, of course, it's contrary to mother's and Millicent's plans.'

'Interest in me?' I was amazed. 'You must be dreaming, why we positively bristle when we're in each other's company.'

'*You* do, I know you think you don't like him, but he doesn't bristle, as you call it. Unless it's because he knows you dislike him and it upsets him.'

'Upsets him? Rubbish. I don't know where you've got this foolish idea from, but the sooner you forget it, the better.'

'I'm sorry I've made you angry. But it's true, I'm sure.'

'But we still haven't solved the problem of Cedric Rothbone, Charles and you,' I said.

'But I don't know whether Charles feels the same about me, do I?'

'No,' I said slowly, 'not for sure, but I've a feeling he does.'

'Really?' Georgiana was joyful again. How turbulent are the emotions of those in love, I thought, in the depths of despair one moment and radiant the next.

'We will think of something, my dear,' I said. 'You won't marry Cedric Rothbone, if I can help it.'

And I had to leave her to change for dinner.

CHAPTER FOUR

During the next few weeks, the family's treatment of me remained much the same, though Georgiana and I were restored to our former friendship. Lady Courtney was hostile and never let an opportunity slip of belittling me. Sir Hugh occasionally called me Victoria, but, on the whole, he seemed to be getting used to coming across me unexpectedly, and the shock he had experienced when first meeting me, grew less each time. Although at times I was aware of him watching me in a strange way.

Bassett seemed cool towards me and I noticed that he paid greater attention not only to Millicent but also to Evelyn Corby. I was annoyed to find that it affected me a little. I was not jealous, I told myself, how could I be when I disliked the man so? Serves him right if he does end up with the simpering Millicent, I thought.

But I could not imagine that a girl like Millicent, with no thought in her pretty head beyond securing a man and making a good marriage, would make a man like Bassett Courtney happy. And somehow, even though I disliked him, I thought he deserved happiness.

Once, when he encountered me in the hall and it was difficult for him to avoid me, I found myself wondering exactly what he thought of the two young women beneath his roof—Millicent and me. And of Evelyn the constant visitor to Courtney Hall.

I was sure, in spite of what Georgiana had said, that he felt much the same about me as I did for him, that the dislike was mutual, for why else should he avoid me ever since the episode in the treasure room. His concern for my welfare, I decided, was merely because he was a good landlord to all the villagers, and I came under much the same category. I was his protégée and he wanted no one to think that he could not look after me as well as his Uncle James had done.

It was strange to think that we had the same uncle and aunt and yet were not related. But some mystery tied me to the Courtneys I was sure of it now. Something to do with my mother, and though I could not ask outright for it seemed to be a closely guarded secret, I was determined to find out one day what it was all about.

'Do you think, Louella,' Bassett said when we met in the hall, the frown never leaving his face, 'that you could find time to come for another ride with me one afternoon, or are you otherwise engaged with Dr Corby?'

'Of course not, Bassett. I should like to come, thank you.'

Naturally, I did not want to go riding with him whilst he was in such a mood, but what else was there to say?

When the master commanded, all must obey.

'Good,' and he strode away without another word.

The proposed ride through the Courtney village this time, took place two afternoons later, but it held none of the pleasure of the first outing we had had together, which Millicent's arrival had spoilt. I felt I would never again be at such ease with Bassett as I had been before that carriage had rolled into view.

Bassett remained morose and hardly seemed to remember that I was with him.

He sat erect and tall on his horse, his brow creased, his mouth a hard line and his eyes filled with some deep emotion I could not read.

It seemed now that I had only Georgiana and Charles as my friends in this household, which I was supposed to regard as home.

We returned to Courtney Hall and I

was more miserable than I had been for a long time, if that was possible for I had not often touched the heights of happiness during my stay at Courtney Hall.

Bassett helped me to dismount and again held me for a moment or two and looked down at me as he had done near the stream on our first ride. But now there was no sorrow mingled with the anger, as I had seen before, now merely anger.

'You have not enjoyed your outing, Miss Lloyd?' The words were harsh.

My temper, for so long held in check, flared uncontrollably.

'How can you expect me to enjoy it, when you have been like a—like a—grumpy old bear? I can't understand you, any of you, except Georgiana.'

And I tore myself away from his grasp and ran from the stables towards the house. It was a long way and soon I was forced to slow to a walk. I risked a glance round to see what Bassett had done.

He was standing where I had left him, staring after me. Though it was too far away to see the expression on his face, I had the impression he was dejected, for his arms hung loosely by his side and his body slumped in a way I had never seen the arrogant Bassett stand.

I shrugged and entered the house. Why should I care what he felt when he had behaved so abominably this afternoon? But I was startled to find that I did care, and I was annoyed with myself for doing so.

Charles and Evelyn Corby were guests once more at the house that evening and now that Georgiana had found I was not in love with Charles and that there was good reason to hope that he was not with me, she lost no time in spending every possible moment in his company, and more often than not in mine also. For I was a good cover for her.

She knew her family would disapprove of her interest in the doctor, and was quite content, for the moment, to let them think that I was the object of Charles' attentions. Consequently, the three of us spent much time together and because none of the others guessed the truth, the idea that a marriage was imminent between Charles and me grew stronger. Georgiana, they thought was merely being a good friend and helping matters along in chaperoning me.

I was amused, for I saw no harm in it, to see that Evelyn was almost beside herself, in her quiet way, at the thought of her brother becoming involved with a girl and nearing marriage. No doubt she not only loved him jealously and possessively, but she realised her own future was at stake. A man's duty was to his wife and future family before his sister, whatever sacrifices she had made for him in the past.

But I thought she still believed she held considerable sway with Charles and that if he mentioned marriage, she would begin her relentless campaign to discourage it.

She had now joined Lady Courtney and Millicent in their hatred of me. And hatred it was now, for there was no mistaking the viciousness in their remarks to me.

They ridiculed my clothes, my hairstyle, my upbringing, even Uncle James, saying he was a weak character who had lived almost in poverty all his life, marrying Virginia Lloyd, a country girl with no birth or breeding. My mother, being her sister, was presumed to be in the same category and consequently, so was I. But they hardly ever referred directly to my mother or my father. Only by such remarks referring to Aunt Virginia, and to home-breakers and such, was I aware that they were really referring to Victoria Lloyd, my mother.

And once I overheard Lady Courtney say to Millicent,

'We shall indeed be fortunate if Dr Corby will marry Louella for she has little to offer any man. You need have no fear of her as a rival for Bassett's affections, I assure you, my dear Millicent. My son has more sense than to fall for a girl of her breeding, unlike his father.'

Such remarks were unbearable at times, and looking back, I can hardly understand why I stood it all. I could easily have run away and found myself a post as a governess. But for some reason I stayed where I was.

Probably I realised that if I crossed the Courtneys too much, I should never keep a governess's post for long, for their power to make or break a person was undeniable.

That evening after the dismal afternoon ride with Bassett, something happened which was to drive all other thoughts out of my head for some time.

We were seated in the drawing-room after dinner, when the gentlemen joined us.

'We have just been telling Charles about

the Courtney dagger, mother,' said Bassett. 'He is most interested to see it.' He turned to Evelyn Corby.

'Millicent, I know, is well acquainted with its history Miss Corby, but perhaps you have not heard of our famous dagger?'

'Lady Courtney has related to me some of its history and the superstition surrounding it, yes, but I have yet to see it.'

'Then you shall,' he turned to his father. 'Since Miss Corby desires to see it, we shall not trouble her to go to the gallery. Perhaps you would fetch the dagger, father?'

'Certainly, my boy, with pleasure.' And Sir Hugh bustled off, proud to have the opportunity of showing off one of his treasures, in fact, the greatest treasure.

Whilst he was gone, the talk centred on the dagger.

'Bassett, of course, being such a strong-minded young man,' remarked Lady Courtney, the pride apparent in her tone when speaking of her beloved son, 'does not whole-heartedly agree with the superstition, Miss Corby. He is too practical to believe in the dagger's powers.'

'I am inclined to agree with him, I'm afraid, Lady Courtney. I cannot see that a jewelled dagger, however beautiful, can have the power to change men's fortunes in the way you have told me. It seems to me that because they parted with the dagger, they brought about their own downfall in believing so strongly in it. They thought disaster inevitable, and so did nothing to prevent it.'

'Very true,' said Bassett. 'Though the people who parted with the dagger cannot have believed the superstition, otherwise they would never have parted with it. Though mother says I am sceptical of its powers, which I am, I would never dream of parting with it, whatever its monetary value.'

At that moment, in contradiction to Bassett's very words, Sir Hugh burst into the room.

'The dagger—it's gone,' his voice rang through the room.

All eyes turned towards him, shocked.

Bassett was the first to recover.

'What do you mean, father, gone?'

Sir Hugh spread his hands helplessly.

'It's just gone from the cabinet.'

Bassett strode from the room and with one accord we all rose and followed him.

'Someone must have stolen it,' decided

Lady Courtney. 'We shall find out who the thief is.' And with a shock I saw she glanced at me.

We reached the treasure room. Bassett was already standing before the glass cabinet staring at the empty black velvet cushion, a puzzled frown on his face.

'Peculiar,' he murmured, 'most peculiar. The cabinet is intact. Not a mark on it, the thief must have found a key.'

He turned to Lady Courtney.

'Mother, you keep the third key. Mine is here,' he held his key in the palm of his broad hand, having taken it from his waistcoat pocket. 'And father has his.'

'I will see if mine is in its usual place.' And she left us.

'Dear, dear, what can have happened?' Sir Hugh dithered. 'The dagger gone, misfortune will befall us now, for certain.'

'Now, father, it may be all right. Don't distress yourself,' said Bassett, though the worried expression never left his face.

'We must question the servants,' said Sir Hugh. 'No one can get into the house and up here without us knowing. And besides, who knew where to find a key?'

Lady Courtney returned.

'My key is here, but it was in a slightly different place to its normal position.' Her voice rang down the long gallery, whilst the Courtney ancestors seemed to listen from their portraits.

'Someone borrowed it and then returned it, hoping it would not be noticed.'

'But who? An outsider would not risk creeping about the house like that,' said Bassett.

'Then it must be someone in the house,' said Lady Courtney, triumphantly.

Millicent moved forward and laid her hand on Bassett's arm raising her troubled eyes appealingly to his face.

'Bassett, dear, I hate to say this, but—but...' she whispered.

'What is it, Millicent?' Bassett's tone was sharp with impatience.

'I saw Louella come out of this room with the dagger this morning.'

'No, no,' I cried. 'I have never touched the dagger.'

I was stunned. How could she tell such lies? I had known her to be my enemy, but this was beyond normal dislike. This was hatred, vicious and cruel.

'Be quiet, girl,' rapped Lady Courtney, whilst everyone else seemed shocked to silence. I felt Georgiana move to my side. But I hardly knew what this dreadful thing was that had happened to me. My instinct told me that my enemies had planned this mischief to disgrace me.

Georgiana took my hand and faced the rest of them.

'Of course she didn't steal it, how can you think such a thing? Bassett, you don't believe it, do you?'

But Bassett did not answer her. He merely watched my face, an unreadable expression on his.

'Georgiana, hold your tongue. How dare you contradict your cousin Millicent and side with that—that mischief-maker?' Lady Courtney almost spat the words at me, she was so angry.

I could not speak. I was so shocked. I would never have believed that anyone hated me enough to play this sort of trick, and to tamper with Bassett's prize possession. It was too much. But at least I knew what sort of person I was up against. Their mind was cruel and merciless, so great was their hatred.

Millicent must be the person, or at least party to it, for here she was telling the deliberate lie, and after all, who but perhaps Georgiana would believe my word against hers?

Upset by the loss of the dagger, Sir Hugh seemed to lose his sense of time and must have reverted to the past.

He twisted his fingers together nervously. 'Victoria, my dear, we must not upset mother so, you must go. Go now, go quickly. Please go.'

He became most distressed. His words made no sense to me, but for his wife, Bassett, and even Georgiana, they must have held significant meaning, for Lady Courtney drew a startled breath and turned pale, whilst Bassett led him gently from the room, and, with Sir Hugh still muttering, took him to rest in his room.

'We had better return to the drawing-room to discuss this unfortunate affair,' said Lady Courtney, regaining her composure. 'And wait for Bassett.'

There was an uneasiness in the room whilst we awaited Bassett's return. As I passed the mirror to take a chair near the window, I saw my face was deathly pale, my eyes frightened, and my mouth trembling. I felt close to tears, surrounded by scheming enemies. But I would not weep, I would not let these people break my spirit. I would fight them.

Before Bassett returned, Lady Courtney began to deride me in no uncertain terms.

'You came to this house, Louella Lloyd, an unwelcome encumbrance on this family. You and your relations have caused nothing but trouble to the Courtney family for many years. Are you never to stop?'

'Perhaps, if I knew what it is my family have done. But I have not taken the dagger. I swear it.'

'Don't make it worse by lying, girl. Why don't you own up and return the dagger? Don't you realise what may happen to us all now the dagger has left the Courtneys? Misfortune will befall us—and the thief. You'll regret it, Louella Lloyd, you'll regret it.'

But her goading was cut short by Bassett's return.

Georgiana dashed to him, she was in tears now.

'Bassett, do something, please. She didn't do it. How could she?'

Bassett put his arm round her, and looked at me over her head.

'Bassett, say you know she didn't do it,' she murmured against his jacket.

'I—I don't know, Georgiana.'

'Bassett,' she flung herself away from him. 'How can you be so cruel? Are you, too, against her?'

And she returned to my side.

'Well, I believe Louella. I'll stand by her, even if you—if you throw me out.'

'That's what we ought to do with *her*,' Lady Courtney indicated me. 'Ungrateful brat. Throw her out, Bassett.'

'No one is to be thrown out, mother, at all. We shall find the thief, never fear.'

'But what will happen to us in the meantime?' Lady Courtney wailed. 'We shall lose all our money, or something dreadful will happen. Look what happens to your father every time he sees her. Look who he thinks she is. How do you think I can bear it?'

And Lady Courtney dissolved into tears in an attempt to persuade her son.

'Get rid of her, Bassett, for my sake. Can't you see she's just like her mother, breaking up our home?'

This was too much. I stood up.

'I don't understand all this talk about my mother. If you won't tell me, how can I? But I am not a thief. I have not touched the dagger. I didn't even know where the keys were to the cabinet. Since you obviously no longer wish me to stay, I will leave at once. I have no desire to remain here either.'

'There you are, you see, Bassett?' screeched Lady Courtney, she was hysterical now. 'She has the dagger, she's trying to get away now. Stop her.'

What did the foolish woman want?

But Bassett took charge of the situation. 'Go to your room, Louella, away from this painful affair, whilst I think what we must do.'

I went. But my heart was heavy with misery. No one, save Georgiana, believed me. Lady Courtney and Millicent had probably engineered the whole thing. Charles and Evelyn Corby had remained silent throughout the family quarrel, and no doubt thought me guilty.

Bassett had admitted he did not know what to think and that was condemnation as far as I was concerned.

The heavy weight of misery I had felt when first Uncle James had told me I was to live here, grew and grew until I felt it would suffocate me. These were unhappy hours indeed, and I could see no brightness in the future.

Night closed in and found me still seated

before my bedroom window, gazing down across the shadowy lawn to the river. I had watched the sun sink lower and lower and the creeping shadows cover the lawn, the shimmering river grow dark and indistinguishable. Now I could hardly see, could no longer draw comfort from my beloved nature. The earth, the trees, the sky, the river never betrayed man as did his fellow beings. Their beauty remained always, giving pleasure, never seeking to destroy man.

But was that true? I asked myself. What of floods, droughts and tempests? Were they not the works of Nature against Man in his weakness?

I sighed. I was certainly alone in my weakness now. Even my brave Georgiana had not come to my room since Bassett had asked me to leave the drawing-room as his mother grew more and more hysterical.

At last I prepared for bed. Even Mary did not arrive to see if I had all I needed as she usually did. Was I to be ignored, shut away in disgrace?

I lay in the darkness and thought over the dreadful happening. Sleep was impossible. But I could not decide who was my real enemy. Lady Courtney? Possibly, for if she took the dagger, then it would not, in actual fact, leave the Courtney possession and she would not be inviting disaster to befall them, as would a real thief. Millicent? The same could be said of her. It was doubtful she would remove it from Courtney Hall. She would merely hide it in her room.

I sat up suddenly. Yes, it would be there, hidden in her room.

Without stopping to think of the consequences, so sure was I that I would find the dagger, I leapt out of bed, found my wrap and stealthily opened the door.

It was not late, I knew, and the rest of the household would still be up. I had plenty of time to search Millicent's room.

I crept along the dimly lit landings until I came to Millicent's grand bedroom. I slipped in quietly. I would have to be careful. A maid might come any time to turn back the bed, or Millicent might retire early.

Though that was unlikely, I thought. She will stay in Bassett's company as long as possible, no doubt taking great delight in pouring her vicious lies about me into his ears.

I began to search methodically through the drawers, the wardrobe and even amongst the bedclothes. I turned towards a jewel case on her dressing-table and opened it. It was large enough to hold the dagger.

I heard a small sound at the door and spun round.

Someone stood in the doorway holding a candle.

I had been caught in the act.

CHAPTER FIVE

The candle flickered and I saw Millicent's gleeful face.

'So, Miss Thief, we are up to our tricks again, are we?'

I did not answer—what could I say?

She turned from the room and called,

'Bassett, are you there?'

'Yes, Millicent,' his deep voice sounded from the hall below.

'I think you should come here a moment.'

And we waited, watching each other,

whilst his footsteps mounted the long stairs—she, with her smile of triumph, me, knowing I had allowed myself to fall into a trap. There was little I would be able to do now to prove my innocence.

Bassett appeared in the doorway behind her, and when he saw me, a foolish figure in my nightgown, inadequately covered by my wrap, bare feet, and hair loose and flowing about my shoulders, I heard his startled gasp.

'Louella, what is the meaning of this?'

'Well, Miss Lloyd, we are waiting,' purred Millicent in deceptively honied tones.

'I—I came to look for the dagger. If Millicent is blaming me, telling lies about me, then she must have taken it herself,' I finished weakly.

I did not think for one moment that Bassett would believe me.

Millicent moved into the room.

'I'm sorry to disappoint you, Louella, but I did not take the dagger. And it seems now, as if you are after my jewels, my paltry few jewels, and you would steal them,' she added pitifully, no doubt hoping to arouse Bassett's sympathy.

Bassett stood aside.

'Go to your room, Louella, and stay there.'

I passed through the doorway close to him.

'You foolish child,' he murmured, so that Millicent could not hear.

I returned to my room, angry with myself. The tears I had so long held in check now flowed.

I, in my foolishness, had confirmed my guilt in Bassett's eyes, I was sure.

I heard the family retire, one by one, and knew that by now they would all know of the latest escapade of the thief. Even Charles and Evelyn Corby would know of it, for it was before they left.

I did not expect anyone to come to visit me now, not even Georgiana. Even she would be doubtful of my innocence having been found in Millicent's bedroom in front of her open jewel case. It was a wonder they had not locked my door.

But I was wrong, for well after midnight, a soft knock came on my door.

'Who's there?' I whispered, and the door opened quietly. I was not surprised that it was Georgiana.

'Louella, you silly goose,' she said affectionately, creeping into bed beside me to keep warm. 'Whatever did you want to go and search for the dagger by yourself for? You know I would have helped you if you had waited. Now you're in a worse pickle than ever.'

'I know,' I said miserably. 'It was the most stupid thing I have ever done in my life. But do you mean to say you still believe me innocent, Georgiana?'

'I want you to swear to me that you did not take the dagger and that you were only searching for it in Millicent's room.'

'I swear it,' I said solemnly. And how solemn I felt. I thought I should never be able to smile again.

'Then I believe you. Now we must think what we can do. I think you are probably right in thinking it is Millicent. I don't see who else it can be. She is obviously terribly jealous of you where Bassett is concerned. Though,' I knew Georgiana was smiling mischievously, 'it might be me because of *my* jealousy of you over Charles.'

'I don't think that for one moment,' I said.

'Well you need not, because it isn't me. But what I can't understand is,' she continued thoughtfully, 'why Charles didn't leap to your defence.'

Although I was plunged in the depths of despair, I saw an opportunity of reassuring Georgiana that Charles was not in love with me.

'Why should he?' I said, 'he does not care enough, even as a good friend, to risk the wrath of the Courtneys by defending me. Why, he probably believes I am guilty.'

'Oh no, surely Charles wouldn't think that. But does that mean he's not in love with you, because if he loved you, he would defend you, guilty or not?'

'I've told you he's not in love with me. That confirms it.'

Georgiana hugged me in pure joy.

'Then, I *might* have a chance.'

'I'm sure you've more than a chance.'

'If only it were so, I should be the happiest person alive. But now, Louella, we must think what we can do to get you out of this mess.'

'There is nothing we can do,' I sighed.

'I shall see Bassett first thing tomorrow and convince him of your innocence.'

'I doubt you can do that. He was there when Millicent surprised me in her room.'

'I must go now, or else I shall be in

disgrace too, and then in no position to help you.'

And with a few more reassurances, Georgiana left.

The night was long and I had never felt so lonely in my life. It was true I had Georgiana's support, but I thought that the belief of a twenty-year-old girl was insufficient against the might of Lady Courtney, Millicent and, most likely, of Bassett, not to mention the Corbys, who, by their silence, must believe my guilt.

Lady Courtney and Millicent had succeeded beyond my wildest fears in disgracing me in everyone's eyes, and in destroying any hope of happiness I might have had.

I remembered Bassett's words about the Smith boy. He had no mercy for dishonesty of any kind, even for a small boy of fourteen, who merely pilfered a few eggs. What mercy, then could I, who was supposed to have stolen his most treasured possession, expect? The answer was obvious. None.

I reached for the miniature of my mother, which always stood on my bedside table, hoping to draw some comfort from the sweet face in the picture, the face I loved and yet had never known. In the early morning light, her features were dim, but as the picture was imprinted on my memory I had no need to look at it to see her clearly. I began to wonder, yet again, what mysterious connection she had had with the Courtney family. Aunt Virginia in marrying James Courtney had undoubtedly introduced the Lloyd family to the Courtneys and it was not unlikely that Sir Hugh and his wife had met my mother. But I could not guess, however hard I tried, why Sir Hugh was so distressed when he was reminded of my mother. To be so affected, he must have known her well. Why, then, could he not give me comfort by telling me about her, the mother I had never known, the mother I so desperately needed now, in my misery.

And so my thoughts took me through to the morning, and I arose, dark eyed and weary from lack of sleep and worry.

I made my way downstairs as usual at breakfast time, and as I stepped into the room, my heart missed a beat. Lady Courtney was waiting for me.

'I am surprised, Louella, that you have the audacity to show your face about the house this morning. A moonlight escape would not have surprised me.'

'I have no need to escape, Lady Courtney, for I am innocent.'

'You will only make matters worse by lying, you foolish girl. You will remain in your room until Mr Bassett has decided what shall be done with you. Your meals will be brought to you, though you don't deserve to be fed from our table. You will not communicate with anyone, least of all Georgiana. The soft-hearted girl may believe in you.'

There was no more to be said, it was useless to argue with a biased woman like Lady Courtney. I left her and returned to my bedroom, where I sat at the window and looked upon the serene world, fresh and pure in the morning sun, and wondered what I had done to deserve this to befall me.

Mary brought my breakfast and though she had obviously been told not to speak to me, she squeezed my hand quickly before she hurried from the room, and I knew that at least I had one other friend in the house.

The morning dragged on. I wondered whether or not Georgiana had been able to keep her promise and speak to her brother on my behalf, though I had little hope of her success in convincing him of my innocence when he had seen me in that ridiculous plight in Millicent's room.

But I was wrong.

At the very time when I had been thinking of her, Georgiana must have been confronting Bassett, for, just before noon, she knocked and entered my room, bringing an unwilling Bassett with her.

'Louella, I have convinced him. See, I said I would.'

I rose and gaped at them both, in wonderment. Could she mean it?

'You tell her, Bassett. I can see she does not believe me. Poor thing, she has been so miserable.' And Georgiana crossed the room and put her arm about me.

I gazed at Bassett and waited for him to speak.

He cleared his throat obviously ill-at-ease.

'Georgiana believes that you would not—could not—do such a thing as to steal the dagger.'

He moved closer and looked down into my eyes as if to read the answer in them.

Innocence or guilt? My eyes would

109

give me away. But I returned his gaze steadfastly. I had no guilty conscience, only fear of my enemies at large in the house.

'And I agree with her,' he finished softly.

'Thank you.' It was all I could reply and all that was needed. As I looked up at him, humbly thanking for his trust in me, I thought how fortunate I was that he believed in me, that I had been spared his wrath. For I still feared him greatly. I suddenly thought how wonderful it would be to be loved by a man like Bassett Courtney and to love him in return. There would be times when he would be angry, or preoccupied with business. But the times when his attention would be wholly concerned with his loved one, what indescribable moments of blissful passion and tenderness they would be.

Bassett turned away.

'I have work to do,' he said gruffly. 'You are to return to normal way of life, Louella. The incident will not be referred to again, unless it is to throw some light upon the real thief. Until that time, it is forgotten.'

And with that command, he left the room.

'There, you see, he's not so bad after all. Say you like him a little more, Louella, just to please me,' Georgiana pouted prettily. 'After all, I have worked exceedingly hard to help you, you might repay me a little by liking my dear Bassett.'

I smiled. She was hard to resist when she put on her coaxing act. I did not wonder that Bassett had believed her in her defences of me. In her own way she was as strong as Bassett, I thought.

'I like him a little more,' I replied obediently. And in that moment I believed it to be true.

Life, as Bassett had commanded, returned to normal, though Lady Courtney and Millicent had fresh fuel to the furnace of their hatred for me. Whenever they caught me alone without Bassett or Georgiana to back me, they continued to upbraid me and almost torture me about the theft, breaking Bassett's rule that it must not be mentioned. And even in company, veiled references of thefts and suchlike were always directed at me, I knew.

I realised now that Lady Courtney's plans for ridding Courtney Hall of my presence by marrying me to Charles Corby were thwarted. And though no doubt she was gleeful at my downfall, in being branded as a thief, she was annoyed to think that I should continue to live at Courtney Hall. Indeed, one of her torments was to say that Dr Corby would not wish to marry a thief and that she doubted whether the Courtneys had anyone of their acquaintance who would be so prepared. It seemed I was condemned to die an old maid.

But her plans for Georgiana's marriage to Cedric Rothbone progressed, to her mind, favourably.

After her elation at her success in restoring me to comparative happiness, Georgiana was now weighed down with her own misery. Though Charles and she were friendly, there was no indication from him that he felt more for her than the fondness of a good friend. She, being in no position to bring about any declaration of love from him, remained in the unsavoury position of being available for marriage to Cedric.

Lady Courtney, with Bassett as a passive ally, suggested the wedding date for the end of September, and duly invited Lord Rothbone and his son to stay at Courtney Hall. It appeared Cedric had no mother, she had been dead for ten years.

As the day of their arrival approached, Georgiana grew pale and listless, and lost some of her beauty. Her mother, noticing the girl's distress, was angry.

'Pull yourself together, child, and be cheerful. Such a picture of misery will not secure you a husband.'

'I have no desire to secure Mr Rothbone as a husband, mother.'

'Come, child. You are being most vexing. I will not have it. You're an ungrateful girl. I can see Louella is having a bad impression upon you.'

These remarks were, as usual, made at the dinner table. But as I kept my eyes firmly fixed upon my plate, I had no means of knowing how the other members of the family were responding to the conversation between Lady Courtney and her rebellious daughter, at least, not until they spoke.

Millicent's high-pitched, whining voice was the first to air her views.

'I'm sure if my mama were so concerned for my welfare and future happiness as is yours, Georgiana, I should be eternally grateful.'

'Then you marry Lord Rothbone's son, Millicent,' replied Georgiana. But her tone these days held none of the fire of youth which was her nature. It seemed that, weighed down by the pressure from her mother, not only her physical health was suffering but also her spirit was finally being broken. It was heartbreaking to watch, and yet I could do nothing.

Or was that true?

Whilst the remarks continued about me, I realised that the time had come when I must carry out my promise first made on that day in the summer house.

I must speak to Bassett.

Bassett was the one person in his household who could over-rule Lady Courtney. And as he did not seem to be doing much to secure Georgiana's happiness, it was up to me to speak to him about it. I trembled at the thought. Never had I felt so frightened of him as I did now when I realised that the only thing that I could do for Georgiana was to face her fearsome brother.

It seemed, in this, that even though he loved her so, she had pleaded in vain against the marriage. No doubt she dare not tell even Bassett that she loved Dr Charles Corby.

Immediately after dinner I followed

Bassett to his study. I must speak out now for Georgiana before Cedric Rothbone arrived, before he had been approved of as a suitable husband, and before plans were too far ahead to be revoked.

At my timid knock, Bassett's deep voice bade me enter, and I saw he was surprised to see it was me. This was the first time since I had come to Courtney Hall that I had deliberately sought his company. At all times I did my best to avoid him, and no doubt he realised this.

'Well, Louella, and how can I be of service to you?'

I felt his gaze to be not without sarcasm, and the smile did not reach his eyes.

'I would like to speak with you about —about Georgiana.'

I swallowed the lump in my throat and tried to still the nervous flutterings of my heart.

He frowned and turned away from me and went to stand before the window. I was thankful, it was easier with his back towards me, without his brown penetrating gaze upon me.

'Well?'

I forgot my calm speech I had prepared. I forgot the fact that I did not want to meet his gaze. I forgot that he was Bassett Courtney, master of Courtney estate, the man to whom I owed everything. I thought only that he was the one person to intercede on Georgiana's behalf.

I ran to him and put my hand on his arm and gazed pleadingly into his face. This was not a feigned expression on my part. I was pleading—pleading desperately for the girl I looked upon as my sister.

'Bassett, please use your influence to help Georgiana. You cannot make her marry a man she does not love. How can you send her to a life of misery with a man she has never met?'

Bassett's eyes darkened, I could see immediately that I had provoked his anger. But there was no drawing back now, what I had to say must be said.

I rushed on, regardless, pouring out all the fears in my heart for Georgiana, were she forced to marry this man.

'I think Georgiana may well have given her heart to someone else. Don't ask me who it is, because I cannot tell you. The gentleman probably does not return her affection and certainly does not know of it. So how can you allow her to be forced to live the whole of her life with a man she may well hate?'

'Since we are talking of arranged marriages,' Bassett said slowly, his unfriendly eyes boring into mine. 'I suppose you count yourself an expert, Louella, since you have seen the results at first hand?'

'W—what do you mean? I know of no arranged marriage. What are you talking about?'

'Don't you?' I thought he seemed surprised. 'Then forget it,' he finished shortly.

'But Georgiana?'

'Louella, don't meddle in things you don't understand. My mother is an excellent judge of character and would wish her daughter no harm, you silly child. I know nothing, nor wish to know, of the world of feminine wiles and arrangements.'

'But has love nothing to do with it?' I asked.

I thought I saw a swift expression of pain, unguarded, distort his face.

'Love?' he said harshly, avoiding my eyes. 'What do you know of love?'

'Nothing, but I certainly wouldn't marry a man I did not love.'

'Wouldn't you, indeed?' And as he looked at me again, I was frightened to see a cruel twist to his lips. 'We may see about that, Miss Lloyd, we may indeed.'

I did not understand his words, but I had no time to venture further upon that line of thought, all I wanted now was Georgiana's happiness.

'Bassett, please,' I tried, pleading once more, but it was no use, and as I saw that, my temper snapped.

'You are the most cruel and odious man I have ever met. How can you stand by and see your sister perish so? I thought you loved her. But I see you have no love in your soul, Bassett Courtney. I pity the woman who marries you.'

Bassett stepped towards me angrily, took me by the shoulders in a vice-like grip and shook me.

'You ungrateful girl. After I brought you here against opposition from everyone, stood by you when you were believed a thief, and you turn on me like that. Get out of my sight, Louella, before I...before...'

He was so angry, I fled from the room in fear.

It was some minutes before I could

control the trembling of my hands and bring the colour back to my cheeks. Then I had to return to the drawing-room. I had to bear seeing Georgiana's unhappy face, knowing that I had failed her when she needed my help, whereas she had saved me when everyone else turned away.

A few evenings later, as it was drawing to dusk we were once more all seated in the drawing-room, but this night we were awaiting the arrival of the Rothbones.

The conversation was light and there were often long silences, whilst everyone seemed occupied with his or her own thoughts.

Lady Courtney was sitting as erect and severe as ever and though she normally kept the flow of conversation going, especially when entertaining guests, such as Charles and Evelyn Corby, who were again, with us for dinner, she was unusually silent tonight. Bassett, when he joined us, seemed restless and every so often would leave his chair and wander listlessly round the room.

I hoped, even yet, that my words might have some effect. Perhaps, he was thinking about them now.

Sir Hugh had long since escaped from the tense atmosphere back to his beloved books, and indeed, it was the best place for poor Sir Hugh to be, for there was no peace or happiness to be found in this room.

Millicent's watchful eyes never left Bassett for long. She would occasionally address him directly, but after several curt replies, she too withdrew to silence for fear of offending the master, whom she badly wanted to attract.

Evelyn, too, had an unusual expression on her face. She was usually remote and held an unchanging face. One could not read the thoughts behind that sulky mouth, and veiled eyes. But tonight, her eyes were her one failure, she could not hide her feelings. And from time to time she would shoot me a glance of hatred unmatched except by Millicent. Even Lady Courtney's dislike of me was hardly so vicious.

I was shocked. I had not noticed before this. I had realised, of course, that she disliked me, but I had not, during the time when I had been so upset by the disappearance of the dagger, taken much notice of Evelyn Corby.

I had not seen her dislike of me grow into such proportions of hatred.

I sighed inwardly. Her feelings were

nothing new. She was only one more to join Lady Courtney, Millicent and probably even Bassett after the display of anger in his study a few days ago. I wondered what I had really done in my short life that deserved the hatred of three, if not four, people.

Charles, too, seemed restless like Bassett, but because he had not the freedom of his own house to walk about at will, he constantly fidgeted and fussed in his chair.

Georgiana and I were seated in the window. I always chose this position for it was the farthest I could get away from the others, and consequently they occasionally forgot my presence and left me in peace for a while. Tonight Georgiana had joined me in an attempt to escape from her family. Her face, ravaged by recent tears, held hardly any of its radiant beauty. She was a poor broken-spirited creature to whom my heart flew in pity. She nervously clasped and unclasped her hands and I could see that the tears were still not far away.

For once I was not impatient with her tears for I agreed that she indeed had reason to weep.

My thoughts were interrupted at that

moment by the sound of carriage wheels on the drive, and Bassett went to the long windows of the room facing the driveway.

'Their carriage is here,' he remarked, and I noticed with surprise that his voice held no anticipated pleasure, he merely stated the fact that they had arrived, and no more.

After a few moments in which the Rothbones entered the house and were met by the butler, they were announced.

With one accord, everyone in the room, except Lady Courtney, rose, and everyone's eyes without exception looked towards the door to greet Georgiana's future husband.

I took her cold hand and I felt her take in a deep breath as she saw Cedric for the first time.

CHAPTER SIX

Cedric Rothbone was a youth of moderate height, pale complexion and blond hair. His stature erect but slim, his hands long and elegant, he held no promise of masculinity. Indeed, his foppish manners and simpering attitude were almost sickening. He wore a perpetual smile on his childish face and, we were to find, he could not converse intelligently, for more than ten minutes at the most. He was selfish and spoilt by a doting parent.

However, when he entered the room, his appearance, though disappointing to me and I am sure to Georgiana also, must have pleased Lady Courtney, for very shortly after their arrival, serious discussion took place between Lord Rothbone and Lady Courtney on the proposed marriage between their offspring.

Cedric planted himself by his prospective bride and there remained, presumably with the intention of getting to know her. But Georgiana would not co-operate. She spoke to him, certainly, but with bad grace, and if the young man had not been so fond of talking of himself, he would no doubt have felt rebuffed by her manner. As it was, he evidently thought he had found a patient and interested listener in her, and launched himself on a chronological account of the life of Cedric Rothbone, Esquire.

Dr Corby and Miss Corby soon left, and I could hardly blame them for they were almost ignored. Lady Courtney gave her whole attention to Lord Rothbone. Millicent seemed to have secured Bassett in conversation and I was certainly not going to leave Georgiana's side whilst Cedric pestered her.

Sir Hugh, of course, remained safely closeted with his books, and how wise I thought he was.

That night when I went to bed I felt even more miserable for Georgiana.

I went to my bedside table to find comfort from the miniature of my mother. But the picture was not there.

I searched my room as best I could, and promised myself a more thorough search by daylight: candlelight was inadequate. But for some reason I felt sure it had been taken, for it had been safely on the small table this morning, I knew, because I looked at it every morning without fail on waking.

Why should anyone in this house wish to take my mother's picture? I was not aware that anyone knew her well enough to want a picture of her. Was it another method of wronging me in some way? Did the thief hope I would make a fuss about its disappearance and cause more disturbance? If that was the case, then I would disappoint them. For, though I was most upset at its loss, I would say nothing to anyone about it.

That night I slept fitfully, and when I did it was to dream of Bassett's angry face close to mine and feel his strong hands gripping my shoulders and shaking me and shouting something about 'you should know about arranged marriages, if anyone does.'

I awoke the next day, miserably aware that there was another day to face, and another, and another, filled with despair.

The days passed. Lady Courtney pushed ahead with the arrangements for Georgiana's wedding. And now another arrangement seemed to be taking shape. The marriage between Bassett and Millicent. Several times, when only the ladies were present, Lady Courtney suggested a double wedding in September. She and Millicent discussed at length how they could bring about a proposal from Bassett.

'He is a stubborn boy,' she said with pride and indulgence. 'But don't worry, Millicent, we shall bring it about, never fear. Why, I must suggest it myself if the poor boy is too shy to do it for himself.

For I am sure that is what is holding him back. I know he holds you in the highest affection, my dear. He just seems to want to hold on to his bachelor state longer.'

And here Millicent would simper and giggle sickeningly.

I would think, on these occasions, how well suited Cedric and Millicent would be, two of a kind.

Georgiana continued to grow thinner and paler each day. Eventually, I became so worried that I thought I would have to speak to Lady Courtney about her. I would not approach Bassett again, for since the day of our quarrel he had hardly spoken to me, and then only with a deep frown and a withdrawn expression in his eyes.

But we were all due for a shock, such a great one that I think it took months for anyone to recover properly, except the person who caused it—Bassett.

We were all seated in the drawing-room as so often when these things seemed to occur. Everyone was there, even Sir Hugh, Lord Rothbone and Cedric too, being guests at Courtney Hall now until the wedding. And also Dr Corby and Evelyn were once again guests for the evening.

Lady Courtney, as always launched herself on the subject of weddings and steered the conversation round to the point of suggesting an alliance between Bassett and Millicent.

'Georgiana is an extremely lucky girl, Lord Rothbone, to have found such a handsome intelligent young husband as your son. You must forgive the child if she seems a little distressed. I think she regrets that her carefree youth is over, and that she must become a woman.'

'The girl is pretty enough if she would take that sullen expression from her face,' remarked Lord Rothbone.

How I kept my temper I do not know, but perhaps it was Georgiana's restraining hand on mine, as if she knew I would leap to her defence and into trouble myself. So I held my tongue, but I was seething with anger that Lord Rothbone could belittle her so.

But for once Charles could not remain silent.

'Forgive me, Lord Rothbone, if I appear impertinent,' and I saw the telltale flush on his handsome face. 'But I think you insult Miss Courtney. She is a beautiful young lady, and I think it is Mr Rothbone who should count himself most fortunate in marrying her.'

I could see it had cost Charles a great deal to say this in front of such a gathering and at the risk of offending his friends and benefactors, the Courtneys, by answering back their guest. But my heart rejoiced that he had at last dared to speak out and in doing so had shown that he cared to some extent at least for Georgiana's feelings. For the first time since the wretched marriage arrangements had started, I saw that Georgiana blushed and looked happy because her dear, beloved Charles had spoken in her defence.

Lord Rothbone looked quizzically at Charles and then, surprisingly, he smiled.

'Why, my dear Dr Corby, I mean no offence to the child. But you must admit she seems a little sad. I think there is beauty beneath that mournful face, and I am sorry that my son seems to be the cause of it. However, perhaps things will change.'

'I am most ashamed of her,' put in her mother. 'She is a most ungrateful girl. I am afraid that Miss Lloyd has an undesirable influence on my daughter. Her whole attitude towards the family is one of ingratitude after we have given her a home. To say nothing of stealing from us.'

'Mother,' Bassett's voice boomed out. 'I said that was not to be referred to again and I meant it. As far as I am concerned, the matter is closed.'

'I am sorry, Bassett, but I think you are letting the girl get away with it. No matter, we will say no more, for I want to talk of more congenial matters. Now, what do you say to a double wedding in September, Bassett?'

'Double wedding?' Bassett's worried frown appeared. 'Between whom, may I ask?'

Lady Courtney laughed.

'Since you are too shy to do your own courting, Bassett my son, it seems I must do it for you.'

A thin voice spoke from the far end of the room.

'Emily, my dear, do you think you should interfere?'

'Certainly, Hugh, and why not indeed?' And she turned back to Bassett.

'Between Cedric and Georgiana, of course, and you—and Millicent.'

All eyes were on Bassett, expectantly. I saw him stiffen in surprise and the words he spoke were full of shock.

'Millicent!'

The way in which he said it, full of incredulity, made me feel a flash of pity for Millicent, the girl who wore her heart so plainly for all to see, and how she must feel at his obvious rejection.

'Who says I am marrying Millicent? I haven't.'

'Why ever not? What better match could you make?'

Lady Courtney looked anxious, no doubt realising that she was up against sterner opposition than with Georgiana. Bassett would not be an easy prey.

'I am not interested in making a "match" as you call it. I shall marry whom I please and when I please.'

'Now, Bassett, we must talk this thing out sensibly.'

'Mother, there is nothing to talk out.'

Bassett crossed the room to stand in front of his mother, no doubt feeling embarrassed that this discussion should take place before so many outsiders.

'Bassett, what possible reason can you have for not marrying Millicent? Don't say you have no affection for your cousin, for I know you have.'

'I do not wish to marry Millicent, and there's an end to it.'

He turned towards her, probably sorry for Millicent as I am sure was everyone in the room.

'Forgive me, Millicent, if I hurt your feelings, but mother brought this about, not me. You would never be happy with me, nor I with you. It would be foolishness.'

Millicent however, was not to acquiesce.

'I could be happy with you, Bassett, very happy.'

Then my pity was no longer needed, for the girl was without pride. She would scheme and plead until she had secured what she wanted. If he was not careful, Bassett would find himself trapped for no better reason than that he did not wish to hurt her feelings.

'Very well mother,' Bassett was saying, 'since you seem so desirous of having both your children enter matrimony on the same day, I will give in. I will marry but I am not marrying Millicent. I shall marry Louella.'

There was a moment's silence as the room vibrated with his words. Then came the violent reactions.

I jumped to my feet and screamed.

'No. Never. I will never marry you, Bassett Courtney.'

Lady Courtney fell into a swoon and Lord Rothbone and Charles rushed to her aid. Sir Hugh pottered over from his corner and clasped Bassett's hand.

'My dear boy, my dear boy, a Courtney and a Lloyd. Fancy, after all these years, a Courtney and a Lloyd.'

The words brought back a vague disturbing memory that I had heard those words before, but I could not place it.

Millicent burst into tears, whilst Georgiana, her own misery forgotten for the moment, hugged me joyfully.

'Louella, you'll really by my sister then. How wonderful.'

'I won't. I won't,' I shouted, like a cross child. 'I won't marry that—that—brute. How can you be pleased Georgiana, when he won't listen to your troubles? How can you wish him on me? I thought you cared about me.'

My temper, my fear of the Courtneys, burst in fury. I felt trapped and, like a cornered animal, I fought.

'I do care for you, and Bassett. That is why I am so pleased.'

Lady Courtney was recovering and was

not going to let such an announcement, even from her masterful son, pass without reprimand.

'Bassett, have you taken leave of your senses completely? Marry *her*. How can you? Think what it will mean to me, your own mother, to have that girl as a daughter-in-law? It's bad enough that she should live here, but to think that she will be the future Lady Courtney is beyond comprehension. After what her mother did, you would do this, to me?'

'I am sorry, mother, that you feel it so. I have made up my mind. Louella shall become my wife whether she likes it, whether you like it, or anyone else likes it, or not.'

And he left the room.

The remarks about my mother did not go unnoticed by me, but I was in no mood to argue that point then. Millicent's tears and anger were directed at me, joined, of course, by Lady Courtney.

'How can you, you vixen? You have schemed this.'

I ignored her and spoke to Lady Courtney.

'Lady Courtney,' I was, for once, not afraid of her. 'I don't want to marry

Bassett any more than you want me to, so I suggest you do everything in your power to stop it. For once, we shall be in agreement.'

'Don't be impertinent, girl. And if you think anyone in this house can dissuade Bassett from this ridiculous idea, then you don't know my son. I am more sorry than I can express, Louella, but when Bassett says something like that, he means it, mark my words. If he means to marry you, however much it may hurt us all, then he will do so.'

I sighed and moved away. I was afraid her words were true. Lady Courtney was a forceful personality. She ruled her husband and daughter, but beside Bassett, her might was insignificant.

The days wore themselves into weeks, and no one could change Bassett's mind. After pleading with him once to release me from his intention of marrying me to be met with a sardonic smile which quickly changed to anger. I left him severely alone and avoided his company. His only answer to my impassioned plea was to place a diamond ring on my finger.

I was not unaware of the great honour

he was bestowing upon me, for I knew that once he married me, for a man like Bassett Courtney, it would be until death.

But why he wanted to tie himself to a woman he did not love, and who almost hated him, I could not imagine. I realised that he had reached thirty without having any serious romantic attachments. But still that did not rule out the possibility that one day he may meet a woman and fall in love with her, a woman who would reciprocate and be far more acceptable to his family.

Sir Hugh and Georgiana were delighted. And this, to some extent, lessened my misery, for in Georgiana's distress at her own forthcoming marriage, if she found happiness in that I was to be her sister, then naturally I took comfort in that, for I found my affection for her growing every day.

I was rapidly becoming fonder of Sir Hugh, also. Occasionally now, since the announcement that I was to be part of the family, he would take me into his study and talk to me about his books. When we were dining or sitting in the drawing-room, I would often find him looking at me long and hard and smiling softly to himself as if dreaming pleasant dreams.

At these times, I had only to turn to see Lady Courtney's furious glances from her husband and back to me, to wonder again what lay behind my ancestry and the Courtneys. Never once, though, did Sir Hugh indulge in reminiscences whilst we were in his study. It seemed that the occasional references he had made to my mother were purely accidental, and he would still absent-mindedly call me Victoria, which did not improve matters.

But no one would enlighten me, and so I continued to wonder.

Because I was so appalled at the thought of marrying Bassett, my mind turned to whys, wherefores, and how I could escape. I thought of running away, but where should I run? Uncle James was now happily established in Canada, so his one letter to me had reported. I certainly had insufficient money to buy my passage out to Canada to find him. And besides, he obviously did not want me, or else I should never have come to Courtney Hall.

I had the ability and education to become a governess, but how was one supposed to start? One still had to live and eat and sleep whilst finding employment. I realised that if I were to apply for a post, any post, the Courtneys, if they wished, could follow me and ruin me wherever I went, because they believed me to be a thief.

I like to think that it was not because I was cowardly that I did not take matters into my own hands and fly from a disastrous marriage. I believe I dealt rationally with the problem in the only way I could.

All around me, girls were forced into arranged marriages with men they did not love, and they led reasonably happy lives. Bassett Courtney, in marrying me, was giving me a home, wealth and position. I should be foolish, I told myself, to run away and probably starve through my own rashness. Besides, they had me in their power over the incident of the dagger. Were I to arouse their enmity further, I should possibly find myself hounded throughout the country as a thief and punishment for such a crime I dare not contemplate.

I remembered Bassett's words over the young boy who had pilfered eggs.

The atmosphere of tenseness did not lessen during the weeks which preceded my marriage. Bassett seemed more morose than ever towards me. Now he turned his attention to Evelyn Corby, and some of her surliness disappeared under the charm which Bassett could exert when he felt so inclined. Millicent still remained at Courtney Hall, still hopeful, no doubt, that Bassett would change his mind. Indeed, the only reason I could think of for his intention of marrying me, was because he wished to escape from Millicent's clutches.

This made me more unhappy for I felt that I was merely being used to get him out of a situation he did not want. I felt that he did not want to marry me at all, but he felt less inclined to be ordered about by his mother so contrarywise, he would marry someone, anyone, of whom his mother disapproved.

And the nearest person was me.

Feelings between my future husband and myself were not improved when he called me to his study one day and told me that he had ordered a dressmaker from London to attend upon me.

'I wish my wife to be dressed as befitting her station. Choose whatever you like, Louella, expense is immaterial. I wish to see you grandly and tastefully dressed. I

138

have no fear but that your taste will be excellent.'

My head rose in proud defiance.

'You have no need to spend money unnecessarily.'

Anger flashed in his eyes. Why is it, I thought, that whenever we meet, sparks fly?

'I order you to have a trousseau of new clothes,' he said between his teeth. 'Do you hear me?'

'Yes, Bassett,' I replied meekly and lowered my head.

I was a fool to rouse his anger so, but it seemed that we awoke in each other some violent emotion and harsh words flowed.

During these days, I found myself more in the company of Charles Corby. I was beginning to notice a subtle change in him. He had always been an interesting companion. But now, often as not, his thoughts turned inwardly and he would sit in silence and melancholy from which I could not rouse him.

I don't know when I first began to hope that these thoughts may be of Georgiana, but as the September weddings approached, his depression deepened and I was convinced that he loved her.

Well, I told myself, as I brushed my long, red hair one hundred times before retiring, if I could do nothing to alleviate my own misery, surely I could help one person in the world I loved, Georgiana, to say nothing of a dear friend, Charles.

As I fell asleep, I determined to tackle Charles the very next day.

But next day, I found I had left matters too long.

On walking to the village to the Corbys' house, I was met by Evelyn.

'Good day, Miss Lloyd,' she greeted me sullenly.

'Good day, Miss Corby. Is Dr Corby at home?'

'No.' At once her eyes gave away the fact that she was jealous of my friendship with Charles. She feared, even yet, that he may marry me, and a wife would oust the sister-cum-housekeeper.

'When will he be in?'

'Charles has been called to London on an urgent conference. Some new discovery has been made, I believe, in the field of medicine, something in which he is directly concerned. I have no idea when he will be back.' She smiled, but the smile did not reach her eyes.

'Possibly not for a month or two.'

'A month!' I gasped. 'But that will be too late.'

Miss Corby bent forward.

'What will be "too late", Miss Lloyd?'

'Oh—nothing—nothing. I was thinking aloud.'

Again she smiled in that humourless way.

'I doubt if he will be back before your wedding, if that is what you're thinking.'

'No—I—of course not.'

I realised my thoughtless slip may complicate matters, but at least Evelyn did not suspect that it was on Georgiana's behalf and not my own that I sought Charles.

I turned away from the Corby house, then I thought.

'But what of his practice?'

Miss Corby seemed lost for a moment.

'I—I think they're sending someone down.'

But in that hesitation, I wondered if she were speaking the truth when she said Charles was away for so long. Was she planning to keep him away from Courtney Hall until I was safely married? It was obvious that she feared I would lure Charles away, and no doubt knowing I disliked Bassett, she thought I would try to persuade Charles to marry me instead.

I left Evelyn Corby watching me from the doorway as I walked down the short drive and along the village street.

It was not often I came to the village, and I could feel the curious glances of the villages upon me. Their smiles of greeting were friendly and respectful befitting those extended to their new mistress, which I was, after all, soon to be.

How could I find whether or not Charles had really gone to London? Whom amongst the villagers could I ask?

Then I knew.

Old Tom, the shepherd in his little hut high on the hillside, would know. Charles visited him every week without fail to attend to Tom's wounded leg which would never heal.

The August sun was hot on my back and the air still and silent as I climbed the hill. High above the village, I could see the farmers moving about their work on the sloping fields, and below in the tiny houses, their wives sang about their chores and children shrieked and played in the sun.

I remembered, suddenly, Bassett's words to me on the day we had gone riding, about the fear of flooding next winter. It was impossible to imagine, here in a sunny, peaceful world, that disaster could ruin all these people spread out below me. I hoped with all my heart that Bassett was wrong.

I reached the shepherd's hut and knocked on the door.

'Come in, come in,' a quavering voice answered and I pushed at the rickety door.

Inside, the hut was dark and dingy, but as my eyes grew accustomed to the dimness, I saw that old Tom kept his shack clean and neat, though it was sparsely and poorly furnished. The old man was stooping over the fire stirring something in a cooking pot.

My eyes took in the table and chair, and single bed tucked away in one corner with two blankets on it. A rush mat covered the wooden floor near the fire, and apart from one armchair, tattered but comfortable, that was the furniture, save a shelf of pots and pans which purported to be his kitchen.

'What be you a-wanting?' he asked, then

straightened up and turned to see who had entered his home.

'Why, it be the young mistress,' and his weather-beaten, crinkled face broke into a welcoming grin.

'Sit yer down, 'ere, missy. It be nice of yer to come and see the likes 'o me.'

I smiled and sat in the old armchair.

'I am wondering if you can tell me whether Dr Corby has gone to London for some time.'

The old man's shaggy white brows met in a frown.

'Why no, missy. But 'ow should I be a-knowing?'

'I know Dr Corby visits you every week and I felt sure he would not leave without letting you know that someone else would be coming.'

His eyes brightened.

'Why, that's so. But maybe the young gentleman had to go off sudden-like and hadna the time to tell any'un.'

'Perhaps,' I sighed for I was afraid old Tom was right.

I rose.

'I'm sorry to have troubled you.'

'No trouble, missy. 'Tis a pleasure to see you.'

And the gentle old man, with all the wisdom of life in his gnarled old face and hands, tender hands which had cared for sheep all their days almost, nodded and smiled at me.

'I'm sorry I canna put your mind at rest about yon man, but if I should see him, I'll say you wish to see him, missy, should I?'

'Yes—yes, please do.'

And after a further short exchange of conversation, I left old Tom.

As I returned to Courtney Hall over the sparkling meadows, even the beautiful countryside could not dispel my depression today. I was annoyed with myself for having left matters so long between Charles and Georgiana. Now it looked as if I had lost the chance.

When I returned to the house, matters were even worse than I had feared for Georgiana met me, once again her face wet with tears.

'Georgiana, my love, what is it?' I asked. 'Come to the summer house where we may talk undisturbed.'

Once more settled in the small place where we seemed to sort out our troubles, Georgiana told me that she had overheard Millicent teling Lady Courtney that if

Bassett seemed set on marrying 'that Lloyd girl' then she should transfer her affection somewhere else, and she mentioned Charles Corby as a possible suitor.

'Mother wasn't taken with the idea at all,' sniffed Georgiana, 'she said she thought Charles, a mere doctor, rather beneath anyone of the Bassett family. And why didn't Millicent leave her marriage plans to her mother and father now. For who was more experienced than the older generation in the choosing of a life partner for their children?'

Georgiana's voice hardened as she added, 'I cannot understand mother's blindness in such matters, having once suffered herself so at the hands of managing parents.'

I put my arm round her shoulders and held her close.

'I tried to speak to Charles today, Georgiana, to ask him outright of his feelings for you, but it seems he has gone to London and won't be back until after the wedding. At least that is what Miss Corby said.'

Fresh tears welled in the girl's eyes, but I was helpless.

'That was good of you, Louella, but I fear he cannot care for me, or else he would have taken matters upon himself to prevent my marriage to Cedric Rothbone,' she said the latter's name with such dislike in her usually gentle voice that I shuddered to think what her life would mean married to a man she detested.

But did I not know myself? For wasn't I to marry a man I hated?

During the last hours I had forgotten about myself in my endeavours to help Georgiana and possibly Charles. As I remembered, a fresh wave of misery enveloped me and if I had not been so firmly averse to shedding tears I would no doubt have cried with Georgiana at our shared unhappiness.

As it was the misery remained inside me, hard and unyielding as I was.

But when all seemed lost and beyond our power, we were surprised that night by a visit from Charles Corby himself.

He came to Courtney Hall after we had dined and evidently asked specifically for me, for when the butler called me from the drawing-room to the hall, Charles came forward and clasped my hands in his.

'Louella, old Tom told me you wished

to see me. Is anything wrong? Is someone ill?'

'Charles,' I cried at the same time as he spoke. 'How glad I am to see you, when did you get back?'

He must have caught my conversation for he asked.

'Back, where from?'

'London!'

'But I haven't been to London.'

'Evelyn said,' I faltered not wishing to distress him if his sister had deliberately lied to me.

'Evelyn?' he said sharply. 'What did she tell you, Louella?'

'Charles, I do not wish to bring trouble between you and your sister. Please forget it. You are here and that is all that matters.'

'No, Louella, I must know.'

I sighed.

'Very well. I called to see you at your home this morning but Evelyn said you had been called to London on business and would not be back before the weddings.'

I saw Charles' gentle mouth set in a hard line and he looked more angry than I had seen him before.

'It seems my dear sister is trying to keep

148

the Courtneys and me apart. She told me that we had better stay away during all the marriage preparations. But come, Louella, what is it you wish to say to me?'

I glanced round the hall, fearful that we should be overheard by a member of the Courtney family.

'We'll take a walk. It is a warm night, and what I have to say must not be overheard.'

I collected my wrap hurriedly and we left the great house and walked through the orchard in the moonlight to the river, where we sat down on the bank, to talk.

'Charles, what I have to ask you is not at all easy, and I beg you to listen with patience and—and kindness.'

I felt rather than saw Charles smile gently in the darkness, and he took my hand in his and pressed it warmly.

'Dear Louella, how could I do anything else?'

'It is best to come straight to the point, I think. What are your feelings for Georgiana?'

I heard Charles' startled gasp in the darkness and his voice when he answered was unsteady.

'I hardly expected to be asked that when

Georgiana is betrothed to be married in less than a month. But since you ask, Louella, and it is *you* who ask, I will tell you truthfully. I love Georgiana with all my heart, but I know that I love in vain, for the Courtney family, however good they are to me, would never consider me as a suitor for their daughter. Besides, I am sure Georgiana could never love me in return.'

I smiled to myself, gaining pleasure from the knowledge that now I could bring the two people in the world I cared about most, together and to happiness.

'But you are wrong, Charles. Georgiana loves you as much, I am sure, as you love her.'

Again he gave a startled gasp, and this time his voice trembled with emotion.

'Louella, do not trifle with me. Are you serious?'

'Charles,' I spoke with mock severity, 'how could you think I would jest about the happiness of you both? You misjudge me.'

'I am sorry, Louella, but what you say is hardly credible. But,' his voice fell with disappointment, 'what are we to do, she is promised to Cedric Rothbone.'

'That you must work out for yourselves.

I cannot arrange for you to meet tonight for poor Georgiana is having to entertain Cedric. But I will tell her of our talk and you must meet tomorrow.'

'Tomorrow,' he sighed softly. 'It may never come.'

'Of course it will, you love-lorn softie.' Then rising I added, 'I must go back to the house or I shall have some uncomfortable questioning to answer.'

Charles and I made our way back to the house and in the driveway before the great doorway, he clasped my hands impulsively and kissed me on both cheeks.

'Louella, you have made me the happiest man alive, till tomorrow, then.'

'Till tomorrow,' I echoed laughing. How love changes a man, I thought.

Charles turned and left me and disappeared down the driveway into the darkness.

I turned towards the house, climbed the steps and stepped into the porch. As I reached for the door handle, I felt myself grasped roughly by the shoulders.

How I did not scream I do not know, perhaps it was too quick, but as I looked up into Bassett's face, the scream died on my lips.

'So, Louella, you go for moonlight strolls with another man less than a month before your wedding? What is the meaning of it, may I ask, or am I to form my own conclusions from the sweet words I heard just now?'

I had never heard such bitterness in a man's voice, nor seen such emotional anger. I feared he would strike me.

I opened my mouth to defend myself, to tell him the truth and then, just in time, I realised I could not.

Bassett would undoubtedly be against Georgiana's marriage to Charles. How could I now betray her and Charles, whatever it cost me? I faced Bassett, my future husband, the man I disliked, and remained silent.

His fingers dug into my shoulders with brutal strength as if he wished to force me to speak. I bit my lip with the pain of his grip, but held my peace. He could beat me for all I cared, I would not give way.

Then suddenly he released me, flinging me from him so that I lost my balance and fell against the wall bruising my arm.

'Go,' he hissed between his teeth. 'Go before I do something I shall regret.'

And he turned and strode away into the darkness.

I watched him out of sight as I had watched Charles.

One man had left me in happiness and one in anger and humiliation. For I had humiliated the arrogant Bassett. Even if he did not love me, he was not the man to take kindly to his fiancée taking moonlight walks with another man. And I blushed with shame that the exchange of conversation he had heard would lead him to believe that Charles and were in love.

I went to bed that night an unhappy creature, for though I disliked Bassett, I did not like making him angry and more unhappy than he obviously already was.

CHAPTER SEVEN

The next day was full of excitement and joy for Georgiana and Charles. When I had gone to her bedroom late that night and told her of my conversation with Charles, it had been all I could do to keep the dear girl from shouting out her happiness aloud and waking the whole household.

The beauty and brightness returned to her eyes and I knew that Charles Corby was the only man for her, and whatever her family said, he was the one who would bring her happiness, never Cedric Rothbone.

She lay down a happy woman in love and when I returned to my room to lay and watch the moonlit ceiling for the rest of the night, thinking of them, I was sure I was not alone in my sleeplessness, for I knew Georgiana, and probably Charles too, would be lying awake thinking of each other and the happiness they would share.

I went with Georgiana the following morning to wait for Charles.

We did not know how or when he would come, but come we knew he would.

We had only an hour or so to wait in the summer house before we saw a boat round the curve in the river and knew by the impatient strokes of the oarsman that it was Charles. Georgiana jumped to her feet and would have rushed to the water's edge to meet him, but I held her back. 'No, wait here. You must not be seen from the house.'

Impatiently we waited whilst Charles drew nearer. He moored his boat and bounded up the path to the summer house.

He hesitated on the threshold as he saw Georgiana.

There was a moment's silence as the two met each other's gaze, for the first time unashamedly filled with love. Georgiana's face broke into a smile and Charles followed suit. With a delighted girlish laugh she ran into his arms and was folded in his loving embrace as if she would never leave it.

With tears in my eyes, I left them together to work out their future. Now I was alone once more, for their world held no place for me. But their happiness left me with a warm glow. I had been instrumental in bringing them together and I must draw comfort from that. As I walked slowly back to Courtney Hall, I felt suddenly very sad that I could never experience such a love—never feel it for a man, nor enjoy the love of a man such as was Charles' love for Georgiana.

My marriage to Bassett Courtney would bind me for ever to a man I feared and disliked.

I crossed the smooth lawn in front of the house and entered the shadow of Courtney Hall, the building which shadowed my life. Would I never be free of its clutches? It seemed not, now.

Bassett was in the hall with Millicent when I entered. His hard glare reminded me of the previous night. And as I neared them, for I could do no other as I passed by to the stairs, Millicent's feline smile preceded some scathing remark, I was sure.

I was not disappointed.

'Miss Lloyd has returned once more from her amorous stroll, I see.'

My glance rested on Bassett. I was surprised that he had confided in Millicent. But it seemed that he was as surprised as I was that she seemed to be of the same opinion.

'But what are those I see sparkling in those fine eyes?' she continued, sarcasm lining her every word. 'Surely not tears from you, Miss Lloyd, or has your lover spurned you, now that you are promised to Mr Courtney?'

'You are misinformed, Miss Bassett. I have no lover, and it would seem unlikely, now, that I shall ever be so blessed.'

And I hurried upstairs, for I could no longer bear their remarks and slurs.

I was truly alone now with no one to turn to, for that night Georgiana left Courtney Hall under the cloak of darkness to elope with Charles.

Georgiana did not want me to help at all in her flight, for she said I would have enough disapproval to bear because I had helped them this far, without being involved in the actual elopement. But I might as well have been there to wish them 'God Speed' for I lay awake in my room listening for every creak in the silent house, imagining Georgiana creeping silently like a shadow down the wide stairs in her dark blue cloak, across the moon-streaked hall, gliding through the huge door out to join Charles and happiness.

Once I thought I heard the soft click of a door and wondered if it were her, but I did not go to see. I might wake the household and spoil everything.

It was not until the early hours of the morning, when I knew that the young lovers would be well away from Courtney Hall, that I fell into a dreamless sleep.

I arose next morning, prepared for the onslaught of abuse which was bound to come my way. It was some time before Georgiana's disappearance was discovered. The family thought she had overslept. But as we were finishing breakfast, we were interrupted by the hasty arrival of Miss Corby in great distress.

She entered the dining-room and ran straight to Bassett. He stood up immediately and steadied her as she flung herself into his arms, weeping hysterically. She had given no one else in the room a glance at all.

'Bassett, oh Bassett, you must help me, please. Charles has left home, gone away,' she raised tearful eyes to look at him. 'I am sure he has eloped—with—Louella.'

I remained where I was, but I could hardly keep the smile from my face. There was the reason for her dislike of me, she had indeed thought her brother and I were in love. She had obviously never considered Georgiana as being the real object of his affection.

Bassett looked at me in puzzlement, above her head.

'Miss Corby, Evelyn,' he said, 'please calm yourself and sit down. As you can see, Louella is still here, she cannot have run away with Charles.'

Evelyn spun round and the shock and disbelief were apparent on her face. She stared at me for a few seconds before sinking slowly into a chair.

'Then—then—who is it? Who can it be?' she whispered mystified.

'Who can who be?' asked Lady Courtney gently, as yet unaware that this was to affect her so nearly.

'Charles has most definitely gone away to be married, for he left me this letter.'

And she held out a sheet of paper to Bassett.

Bassett read the letter with interest.

'You are right, but he gives no indication as to whom he is to marry. Have you no idea, Evelyn?'

'No—no,' she glanced at me, 'not now.'

And she lowered her eyes, possibly ashamed for jumping to conclusions.

Then I found Bassett looking at me, his voice hardened from tones of solicitude with which he had addressed Evelyn, when speaking to me.

'Have you any idea, Louella, as to whom Charles' wife is to be?'

I realised I could not lie. There was no point. The couple would be safely away, and as it was obvious I was involved, it would be better to get it over with immediately.

'Yes, I have.'

The room buzzed with exclamations.

'Then would you be good enough to tell us what you know?' Bassett boomed.

I sat very erect in my chair as I made the startling statement.

'Charles has eloped with Georgiana.'

'What?' Lady Courtney gave a little scream and promptly fainted.

Sir Hugh seemed stunned, hardly to have taken the news in. Bassett, Millicent and Evelyn were all too astonished to move, so I sprang to assist Lady Courtney.

'Bassett,' I commanded, 'please ring the bell for Mary.'

He did so in a daze. I knew that any moment their anger would burst forth with me as the recipient, but Lady Courtney's swoon was far more important.

Bassett helped me then to carry his mother to the sofa and eventually she recovered. But I was sure the swoon was genuine for she was really distressed and looked pale and ill. I felt a moment's pity for the woman, for it must be a shock for any mother to hear such news.

'Oh Bassett what are we to do?' she

held out her hand to her son, seeking his reassurance and strength.

'The shame of it, the shame of it upon the Courtneys. How could the girl do it? How presumptuous of Dr Corby to foist his attentions upon an impressionable young girl like Georgiana.'

And she fanned herself vigorously.

Evelyn continued to dab her eyes and sniff. I was sure that she had merely transferred her dislike from me to Georgiana, for now she had indeed 'lost' her brother. I could not feel any pity for the selfish, moody young woman. I could only wish that Charles would find the happiness he so deserved with Georgiana.

I turned to look at Bassett. What was he thinking about the affair, I wondered, he had said little yet.

The expression I saw on his face startled me. He was looking directly at me and the smile on his face showed clearly that he was not seriously perturbed at the elopement of his young sister.

'Bassett,' I said hesitantly, 'you are not angry?'

'No—not angry,' and he added softly, 'only relieved.'

Before I could ask what he meant, he

had turned away to give further comfort to Evelyn, who was very much in need of it.

Relieved? I was puzzled. Why? Was it because Bassett was thankful now that Georgiana was not to marry Cedric Rothbone? My brow wrinkled with perplexity. But he had refused pointedly to take steps to prevent it as I had begged him. Surely, if he had thought it against Georgiana's interests he would have opposed the marriage plans? And undoubtedly the sway Bassett wielded would have been sufficient to quash the marriage. This was the only thing I could think of, for I was sure his relief was nothing to do with me, and the fact that I was not marrying Charles.

I bent to help Lady Courtney, who was still suffering from shock and mortification.

But my help was rebuffed.

'Is this another of your schemes, Louella Lloyd, to discredit the Courtney name further?'

'I did not make them fall in love.'

'Love? Pah, what do you know of love?'

I felt that now the others in the room were listening, for Lady Courtney's hysteria had attracted their attention. There was silence in the room as they awaited my answer.

'Very little, I fear, from my own point of view, but if you had seen them together, Lady Courtney, you could not deny the love between them. Surely you would not deny Georgiana such happiness?'

'It is not for you to tell me what I should or should not do. But for you, I believe my daughter would have made a good and suitable marriage to Cedric Rothbone.'

'Now, mother,' Bassett's tone was indulgent. 'It is not fair to blame Louella.'

He turned to me.

'Mother must blame someone and since the guilty pair are out of reach, you seem to be the nearest,' and I imagined I heared him mutter beneath his breath, 'as always.'

I was grateful for Bassett's defence of me, and for once I warmed to him. Perhaps there was a spark of feeling for his inferiors somewhere beneath that aloof air.

'Bassett, I must explain...'

'Not now, Louella, later. Tell me later.'

And he turned back to his mother.

'Come now, mother. I think you should rest. This has obviously upset you.'

And he helped her up and put his arm about her gently.

'Bassett, oh Bassett, what have I done to deserve such erring children?'

And with renewed vigour she wagged her forefinger in Bassett's face.

'You're no better, Bassett Courtney, than your disobedient sister—insisting on marrying that—that—'

Words failed her and she could find no adjective insulting enough to apply to me.

As Lord Rothbone and his son went for an early morning ride and breakfasted later than the rest of us, they had missed hearing the news. The unpleasant task of breaking it to them fell upon Bassett. I did not envy him, for I deduced that Lord Rothbone's cold eyes and thin lips were a sign of violent temper if thwarted.

Later, Bassett told me of his interview with father and son in his study.

'I thought for a moment, Louella, he would strike me,' he said speaking of Lord Rothbone, 'he was so angry, he turned purple. But Cedric merely smiled and shrugged. I doubt very much whether he had any deep feeling for Georgiana at all.'

I felt his dark eyes upon me and hesitatingly, I met his gaze.

'I must admit you were right, Louella,' he said softly. 'Cedric would never have made her happy. I regret I did not move to stop their marriage.'

I smiled, ready to forgive him now that Georgiana's happiness was secure.

'You cannot be expected to understand the desires of a woman's heart.'

'And your own, little Louella?' His tone dropped so deep and soft that I scarcely heard. I was disconcerted. I answered hastily, afraid somehow of being trapped.

'Mine?' My voice was slightly shrill with nervousness. 'My heart is not captured, I am thankful, for it seems it can bring unhappiness as easily as happiness.'

Bassett's tender tone and gentle look disappeared.

Whatever answer he had looked for, I had not given it. He changed the subject and the moment when we might have found some sort of mutual understanding was lost. I acknowledged the fault to be mine.

My prickly pride would get in the way and spoil things.

Had Bassett been trying to find out

whether I was heartbroken at the loss of Charles to Georgiana? And if so, what was his motive?

'I fear we shall have trouble this winter, Louella,' Bassett was saying, 'and since by that time you will be my wife, it will necessarily involve you. So I think you should be warned.'

He had turned away from me and gone to stand before the window to gaze at the long slope down to the rippling river flowing serenely on its way to join the ocean.

'How do you mean?'

'Do you remember, when we were taking that ride together, the first one, the day Millicent arrived, I spoke about droughts and floods?'

'Yes, I remember.'

'It seems that the fears then voiced by the old men in the village are becoming more widespread. The weather prophets are foretelling a very severe winter with heavy snowfalls.'

Bassett turned sharply and looked at me.

'Which means that the melting snow will probably cause the river to flood.'

'Oh Bassett, how dreadful. Whatever

166

will the villagers do, their homes will be flooded?'

Bassett crossed the room and stood before me again. He put his hands on my shoulders and looked down into my upturned face.

'Louella, you are good for me. Remember that, whatever anyone else may say.'

At such a compliment, I blushed and let my eyes drop. I felt Bassett's lips brush my hair in a tender kiss.

I was startled. I had expected no such display of emotion from the master of Courtney Hall.

But as he turned swiftly away and resumed his earnest conversation on his plans for the victims of the flood, should it occur, the moment was forgotten and afterwards I wondered if I had dreamt it all.

'The occupants of any house threatened by the flood would have to come up to Courtney Hall, of course, for being on higher ground it is most unlikely that we shall be affected at all.'

'We could turn the ballroom into a sort of dormitory for the men, and most of the women and children could probably be accommodated in the bedrooms. There are a vast number in the north and south wings unused.'

'That's a good idea, Louella, I had not, I must admit, got as far as thinking about actual places for their sleeping quarters.'

He paused and his tone hardened.

'We shall no doubt meet with opposition from my mother. She feels it lowers the authority and position of the master of Courtney to give shelter to his workers.'

I remained silent, though I think Bassett expected an answer. I did not wish to embark upon making derogatory remarks about his mother.

'But she will have to be told,' he said firmly, and I smiled inwardly at his tone, knowing that she would, indeed, be told.

The matter of the flood was not spoken of for some time after this conversation had taken place, for the summer days of late August were so bright and peaceful that the world seemed as if it would never snow or rain again. It was difficult to think of winter weather and rushing water, when strolling by the lazy river under cloudless skies.

Preparations were well under way for our wedding, and came the day when the dressmaker from London, specially hired by Bassett, arrived with samples of material and patterns for my choice of gown.

I had to choose it alone and no one else, except the maid who was to help me dress on my wedding morning, was to see it, but the dressmaker and myself.

A suite of apartments had been set at his disposal, for he had not only to make my wedding finery and a whole trousseau of clothes for me, as Bassett had ordered, but other members of the household, the bridegroom included, demanded a new set of clothes.

I had never seen such material or such beautiful patterns. I was lost. I turned to the little man at my side.

'Mr Lewisson, I am overwhelmed. I have never seen such grandeur. I really don't know what to choose. Please help me.'

He was a kindly little man with a slight foreign accent. He was unassuming, but reassuring. I felt he knew I was unused to the position in which I found myself, and he was sympathetic.

His long, delicate fingers, used to stitching fine garments with endless patience, guided the flying pencil over sheet after sheet of paper, designing, suggesting, guiding my choice of wedding dress and fine gowns.

'Might I suggest, madam,' he murmured, 'that for your wedding gown you should wear a unique gown, one which we will design together, you and I. An exquisite gown.'

The dress he drew seemed so complicated to me that I could not really imagine how it would look. It was all pleats and trains and drapes. The other gowns were more simple, amongst them being a high-necked, long-sleeved, tight fitting day dress in pale blue; two afternoon dresses with plain skirts and over dresses cut in princess style draped in all manner of directions, and decorated with ribbons and lace; a summer dress in lemon; a high-necked dress with a printed flower pattern. There were three evening gowns of different colours and materials, my favourite being in emerald green, low neckline and embroidered with sequins.

'How can I thank you, Mr Lewisson?' I said, gratefully when we had finished. 'The garments you have chosen and designed are lovely, but I fear I cannot do justice to them.'

'You are too modest, madam, your

gentle beauty will be richly enhanced by these clothes. You will not displease your groom, I guarantee.'

I coloured slightly, for the poor man was naturally under the impression that my sole intention was to please Bassett. Perhaps, in some measure, he was right for I certainly had no wish to displease him—I was too frightened of his wrath. But I was not, as a young bride should be, anxious, to the exclusion of all else, to captivate my bridegroom completely.

I knew I had not the power to do so, had I wished.

The days flew by and the house became alive with activity in preparation for the great day. There were over a hundred guests to be invited for what was to be one of the biggest weddings in the country.

Lady Courtney, over-ruled by her wilful son in the choice of his bride, had won her own way in having a grand wedding, and because I had no family to give me the wedding, it fell to the Courtneys, who, thwarted in their right to give Georgiana a grand wedding, revelled in their son's marriage plans.

Bassett, I noticed, kept out of all the

arrangements and left them entirely to his mother. And she, in her element, was a great deal easier to get along with from my point of view. But each time she remembered exactly who it was that Bassett was marrying, obviously it spoilt her complete enjoyment of the proceedings.

But, I must admit, in fairness, she was a little kindlier disposed towards me.

I could not help feeling that this came about because Millicent had left Courtney Hall for a short while.

Her long stay had come to an end, and she had returned home on the pretext of completing her own preparations for the wedding. But she intended, she made it clear, to resume her stay at the Hall shortly before the day of the wedding. But I believed that with her vicious tongue removed from pouring tirades against me into Lady Courtney's ear, and with the latter gleefully occupied in being the pivot of the arrangements, I was less hated than previously.

Sir High, bewildered as I with all the preparations, confided to me that he was 'as pleased as punch' that Georgiana had escaped the clutches of that 'simpering whippet Cedric.'

'I don't know how Emily could have chosen the boy for her, really I don't. Why, Victoria, Emily seems to have no idea of what is best for her children. Indeed she doesn't.'

And he sighed sadly.

By this time, I had grown used to his calling me Victoria. I no longer worried about it, though at times I was still curious to know why he did.

The wedding date was set for the nineteenth of September and as the day neared, the weeks seemed to fly past even more quickly.

On the afternoon of the fifteenth, Lady Courtney and I were seated in the drawing-room, discussing final plans for the day—at least, Lady Courtney was instructing me in the proper manner in which to conduct myself amongst the important guests who were to be present.

'Although you are the most important person in the gathering,' she paused and I thought that she was probably reflecting upon the undesirability of my person being the central character. However, she continued.

'It is not expected of you to carry out onerous duties on such an occasion. Your main task will be to appear shy, happy and polite to all your guests. Wedding day nerves are indulged by all, even Lords and Ladies, though you are not expected to weep, to blush excessively, or to show your nervousness by any outward sign.'

At this point, her conversation was interrupted by the sound of the arrival of a carriage.

Lady Courtney rose.

'Now who can this be arriving at such an hour?'

I rose from my seat when Lady Courtney did so, but did not follow her to the window. However, when I heard her gasp of surprise, I moved a little nearer to try and see who had arrived.

Lady Courtney turned from the window, her face white, her eyes wide and startled.

'Fetch Bassett—I'll find Sir Hugh,' she added as an afterthought. 'It's Georgiana—dared to come home.'

I flew from the room. I would have liked to have gone straight to welcome the couple, but I knew Lady Courtney needed Bassett's help. She was not sure what reception to give her wayward daughter. Perhaps she had not thought that Georgiana and Charles would ever appear at Courtney Hall again. Certainly by the look on her face, she had not prepared herself for such an event.

I knocked on Bassett's study door.

'Come in.'

I opened the door and entered noiselessly.

Bassett was working at his desk, bending over a sheaf of papers. His mouth was set in a hard line, his fingers tapping the desk with impatience. Something in what he was reading was disturbing him.

I was sorry for Georgiana and prayed she had not caught her brother in a bad temper.

Bassett looked up and some of the hardness left his face.

I smiled, uncertainly, and saw his face relax even more.

'What is it, Louella?' he asked, not unkindly.

'Georgiana and Charles have returned.'

Bassett frowned. Fear stabbed at my heart. Surely he would not turn them away?

'Does Lady Courtney know of their arrival?'

'Yes.'

'And what did she say?'

'She—she sent me to find you.'

Bassett merely grunted and rose.

'Come, then, Louella, we shall meet the runaway pair. And since you and I are betrothed, you shall take my arm.'

And he crooked his arm, and offered it to me.

I wondered what game he was playing. Shyly, I put my hand on his arm and we left the study and went to the front door where Lady Courtney and Sir Hugh were already waiting. The door had not been opened and I knew Georgiana and Charles were waiting fearfully on the driveway.

Bassett opened the huge door. I glanced up at his face. He wore a stern forbidding frown.

We stepped out and stood looking down on Georgiana and Charles, whose eyes went straight to Bassett as if trying to read their fate, for they knew with whom it rested.

Though I smiled warmly in their direction, they were not looking at me. Drawn by their regard, I turned to look at Bassett myself. His expression had not altered.

My heart sank. Surely this callous man was not going to turn away his own flesh and blood? Was there no love in him for his own sister even?

'Well, Louella,' Bassett said softly, so that no one else could possibly hear, 'and what is our reply to this entreaty for forgiveness?'

'Welcome them home, Bassett, please.'

'Do you ask that as your wedding gift?'

'Gladly.'

He smiled suddenly, and again the sun shone on a grey world.

'Then we shall.'

He raised his voice.

'Welcome home, Georgiana, welcome home, Charles.' And he stretched out his right hand to them.

Georgiana and Charles leapt forward. Charles to clasp Bassett's hand and Georgiana to fall, almost weeping with joy, into my arms.

All this while, Lady Courtney and Sir Hugh had stood behind us. I could not know what they were thinking, or what their wishes were, but following our lead, Sir Hugh came ambling forward to bestow kisses on his daughter, and Lady Courtney allowed herself to be greeted dutifully by Georgiana and her new son-in-law.

The happiness of the reunion with my dear Georgiana and Charles, the joy with which I heard of their marriage, their short honeymoon and their excited plans, was soon overshadowed by another arrival at Courtney Hall.

The next morning Millicent returned to Courtney Hall in readiness for the wedding.

The easier relationship which I had enjoyed briefly with Lady Courtney ceased immediately. Millicent's treachery was at work again, and it affected not only Lady Courtney, but also Bassett, for he hardly spoke half a dozen words to me from the moment of Millicent's arrival until our wedding day.

CHAPTER EIGHT

My wedding day dawned as perfect as any bride could wish for. From my window, I watched the fingers of early morning sun creep across the lake and light the glowing autumn colours on the woodland slopes beyond. The gentlest of breezes softly whispered across the grass, rippling it like soft waves on a green ocean. Even the birds sang a dawn chorus, solely for my benefit.

I was awake early and occupied with my own thoughts when Mary brought my breakfast on a tray.

Courtney brides, even unwelcome ones, were treated with tenderness and indulgence.

'It's the most beautiful day, miss. Aren't you lucky?'

I smiled wryly, but agreed with her. The girl was as excited as if it were her own wedding day.

But how could she know that this was the day I had dreaded for weeks? This meant, for me, the end of all freedom.

Later, as I dressed, I noticed the slight colour in my cheeks, the brightness of my eyes only enhanced my appearance. These outward bridal signs were not caused by happy anticipation, but by fear, cold and reasoned.

I feared the final bond which bound me irrevocably to the Courtneys.

The mirror told me I looked as well as most brides—would that my heart matched my appearance, I thought.

The wedding dress was a work of art on the part of the little dressmaker. The bodice had a waistcoat front of finely pleated satin with delicate lace flounces on the sleeves and a stand-up collar. A flower-sprigged brocade formed an overdress which draped itself over the bustle and fell in soft folds to a train. The delicate veil was held in place by traditional orange blossom forming a high headdress.

Mary was my only companion that morning, for no one must see my bridal array until I left my room on my way to church.

Mary fussed round me, and I was grateful for her excited chatter.

Ready half-an-hour before I had to leave, I persuaded her to go and get ready herself.

'Are you sure, miss? I don't like leavin' you, really. You look—well—nervous, miss.'

I smiled. Perhaps Mary guessed a little of what I was feeling, but did not like to put it into words.

'Mary, you have helped me enormously —but I am perfectly prepared, now. Off you go or you'll miss the service.'

Alone once more, I stood at the long window of my room. This window, at the back of the great house, looked upon nothing of the flurrying carriages and coaches, which I knew were leaving at the front of the house. My panorama was peaceful, sunlit countryside. The trees, still clothed in their autumnal leaves, rustled gently and the river glimmered in the sunlight.

The countryside was happy and so beautiful that I felt a lump in my throat.

I thought of Aunt Virginia and Uncle James and longed for their comforting presence on this dreadful day. My letter to Uncle James, an impassioned plea for his help, for his permission to join him in Canada, lay unposted in my writing bureau. Later, I should destroy it. Every day, I had tried to find the courage to send it. But somehow, the pride which held my tears in check, also forbade that I should beg and plead for favours.

I was already the unwilling recipient of too many Courtney favours.

For some strange, twisted reason of his own, Bassett had demanded that I married him. I was certain, now, that he was using me as a means of avoiding marriage with Millicent; a means to avoid hurting the girl in a blunt fashion; a means to thwart his mother's plans; and perhaps even a means of quelling the rebellious spirit of the orphan who had arrived, unwelcomed, on his doorstep.

To rebel against a marriage which promised a reasonable security and a high standard of living was unthought of, especially one which led to the luxurious living of the mistress of Courtney Hall. But what of happiness?

In that half hour as I waited in my bridal gown, I firmly believed that the happiness I had known in my life when I had lived with Aunt Virginia and Uncle James was far behind me, and that I should never taste such happiness again.

Suddenly, I longed for Georgiana's company, and Charles' too. They had some affection for me, I thought. I forced myself to forget my self-pity and to count my fortunes.

I smiled wryly to myself.

At least plain Louella Lloyd was not to be left an old maid. At least I was entering the honourable state of marriage. I would be well established and comfortable.

But still—I could not forget my dislike of the man I had to marry.

I shuddered to think that I had to submit to this man's every demand, and I dreaded my wedding night.

A gentle tap on the bedroom door disturbed my troubled thoughts.

' 'Tis time for you to come down, now, miss,' Mary's excited face peered round the door. 'There be only Dr Corby waiting to take you to church.'

I picked up my bouquet of red roses, carefully, whilst Mary came forward to adjust the gossamer veil over my face.

Slowly, almost regally, we descended the stairs.

Charles stood in the hall, resplendent in his new suit. As I had no relation near, Charles was to give me away.

His face was sober. I wondered what could be amiss. My heart lurched. Was something wrong between Georgiana and him. There was such an odd expression in his eyes.

Mary slipped away down the passage to hurry across the field to the little church standing in the Courtney parklands, only a short distance from the Hall.

Still Charles did not speak but continued to stare at me.

'Charles...' I began hesitantly.

He jumped visibly.

'Louella—forgive me—I was beginning to wonder if you were real. My dear, I never realised how beautiful you would look.'

'Bless you, Charles. But I don't need flattery to give me courage—I am quite resigned.'

A small frown crossed his face, then he smiled.

'Dear Louella, who has given me so much happiness with my dearest Georgiana, when will you learn to distinguish truth from flattery? But come, we must away. Your golden coach awaits, princess.'

And so, with Charles' strange mood dispelled and his buoyant spirit restored, we left Courtney Hall—I for the last time as Miss Louella Lloyd.

It seemed that all the residents of Courtney village were milling round the church. They waved, smiled and shouted greetings and good wishes. I was moved by their friendliness.

The organ notes, muted and solemn, met us as we alighted from the coach and stepped into the porch.

The church door opened and we waited briefly whilst Georgiana, as my matron of honour, took her place behind us.

I could not help a stab of envy as I

saw the loving look which passed between Charles and Georgiana, and their quick touching of hands.

A stir of expectancy ran through the packed church as the organist strode purposefully into the Bridal March. The congregation rose as we entered through the west door and walked solemnly up the aisle.

I kept my eyes fixed firmly on the Altar, far away under the glowing stained-glass window.

We reached the steps, the vicar moved forward to meet us and I felt Bassett move to my side.

All my life I had dreamed of this moment when I would arrive at this place, look up and meet the eyes of the man I loved.

But that was my dream.

And this was reality.

I had arrived, but I did not look up to meet Bassett's eyes. I kept my gaze straight ahead and met the kindly eyes of the ageing vicar.

I have ever since regretted that I did not greet my bridegroom in the customary way, for perhaps then we might, in that solemn, awe-inspiring moment, have found a mutual understanding.

But my foolish stubbornness once more prevented me from displaying any of the normal reactions of a happy bride.

I would not disgrace the Courtneys with sulkiness, but neither would I pretend to feel that which I did not.

And so the service began. The beautiful words flowed on, ringing through the sunlit, Holy place in the vicar's deep tones. I think I made a silent prayer that perhaps one day, the vow I took now would cease to be the mockery it was.

I understood the feelings of numerous girls and women who had stood thus, at a stranger's side, a man chosen by her parents and who had to promise to 'love, honour and obey' him until death.

The service seemed to be over very quickly and we were stepping into the bright sunlight once more, now as man and wife. I smiled and acknowledged the greetings of our guests and the villagers, but though I felt Bassett's eyes upon me from time to time, not once would I glance in his direction. The only acknowledgement I made of his presence, in fact, was my hand upon his arm.

The next few hours were to me a blur

of faces, a cacophony of voices wishing us happiness, and a mountain of food at the grand banquet little of which I felt like eating.

Bassett had decided that we should not leave the estate for a honeymoon, for there was a great deal of work on hand for him with the harvesting of his lands. We were merely to take up immediate residence in the suite of rooms which had been redecorated and furnished as our own home. Though, naturally, Bassett, as unofficial master of Courtney, would continue to direct his business from his study—the hub of the Courtney estate.

I had never in my life seen such grandeur as was displayed at my wedding. The Courtneys had certainly spared no expense, neither had the guests, it seemed, in their dress.

Millicent looked really beautiful for she wore a gown of midnight blue satin, the slim fitting accentuating her tiny waist. The dark colour enhanced her fragile, fair beauty. Though I knew I looked as well as I could in my wedding dress, I could not help feeling inferior beside Millicent. I wondered whether or not Bassett was making a comparison and realising how much more justice Millicent would have done to my gown. Perhaps, even now, he might be regretting his hasty decision.

At last the exacting day was over and as I stepped out of my finery in the dressing-room adjoining the bridal chamber, an involuntary shudder shook me as I pictured the years of misery which lay ahead of me. Marriage, so I believed, was sacred and for ever. I felt ashamed and guilty to think that our marriage was a shallow tying together of two people who felt no love for each other. But, I comforted myself, so many marriages of convenience lacked true love, at least at the outset. Some, luckily, grew to love, but for every one that did, there was certainly one which did not.

I was weary with the day's ceremonies, tired of being looked upon as the happy, blushing bride, when, in fact, I was inwardly still seething with anger against the man who had brought it about—Bassett Courtney.

With Mary's help once more, I changed into the finely embroidered nightgown. Now we were in the suite of rooms prepared for Bassett and his bride. Bassett had arranged that we had separate but adjoining bedrooms. So it was that I sat in my bedroom, after Mary had left me, fearfully watching the communicating door which I knew would open.

The room was tastefully decorated and furnished in the luxurious style typical of the Courtneys, and the bed, from which I kept my frightened eyes averted, was ornamented and heavily quilted with fine, embroidered silk.

A gentle tap sounded on the communicating door and without waiting for a reply, it opened and the master of Courtney Hall stood there.

It seemed an age that we stared at each other, Bassett with a cold mask of indifference on his face—I showing my fear plainly.

He came towards me slowly and I felt panic surge up inside me, but I willed myself to calmness and met his gaze steadfastly.

Bassett stretched out his hand and touched my cheek tenderly in a caress. I was surprised at a display of gentleness from him, but still the hard expression on his face remained.

'Poor child,' he said softly, 'forced to marry a man you despise.'

It was not a question but a statement

and I did not contradict him.

He touched my hair and his hand rested lightly on my shoulder.

'I make no further demands upon you, Louella,' he said, his voice strangely hoarse, as if he were suffering stress, 'until such time as you might—wish it.'

Abruptly he turned and left me, and the door to his room closed behind him.

The emotions of the day, this last unexpected act of gallantry by Bassett, were too much to bear.

I fell into bed. And I, who never wept, sobbed myself to sleep.

Life at Courtney Hall began to revert to normal, that is, in most respects. I was treated as I had been when I first arrived. There were slight differences, of course.

I was now Mrs Courtney—though in name only—and the servants and villagers treated me with the respect which my newly acquired name demanded.

Millicent, a frequent visitor to the Hall, was hardly ever absent from it for long. She and Lady Courtney still derided and scorned me whenever possible, so that I avoided their company as much as I could. This was easier than before, now that Bassett and I had the west wing of the great house as our own suite of rooms, though Bassett used them little.

I, on the other hand, was glad of a means of escape and my rooms were my castle.

Georgiana and Charles came to live at Courtney Hall eventually as life in the Corby house, with Evelyn, began to put a great strain upon their marriage. The Courtneys had now forgiven Georgiana and Charles for their elopement and had in fact accepted Charles completely. So the east wing of the Hall was put aside for their use. My friendship with them in those lonely days was, I believe, the only thing which saved my sanity. But I could not presume too much on their time for a young couple so much in love needed to be alone, and as Charles was fast becoming the most popular doctor in the surrounding district, their leisure moments were few.

I hardly saw my husband for when he was not engaged in the affairs of the estate he delighted in accompanying either Millicent or Evelyn on carriage expeditions or riding.

Never once did he ask me to go with him. Never once did he give any explanation of his activities. He seems to delight, I thought angrily as I watched Bassett, Evelyn and Millicent ride away one afternoon, in ignoring me now. Safely married, he can now flirt with whom he pleases.

I felt the tears prick my eyelids. It's not that I'm jealous of them, I told myself, for jealousy surely only arises from love, but to be spurned thus—what must the villagers be saying?

But it was probable that the villagers, if they did see him in the company of either Millicent or Evelyn or both, saw nothing wrong, for was not Millicent his cousin and Evelyn his sister-in-law almost? And no villager, all of whom without exception I knew worshipped their young master, would think ill of Bassett until it hit them in the face.

During the next few weeks I passed through a dreadful time of loneliness and depression.

Married to a man I loathed, branded by his mother as an unwanted burden and a thief, and always, lurking in the background, was the mystery surrounding my mother and the Courtney family.

Lady Courtney still retained full charge of the household management and there was little for me to do.

It was during this time that I became closer than ever to Sir Hugh. During the warm days of autumn he would often, when he could tear himself away from his books, take walks with me, usually along the river bank.

He was a gentle man and he delighted in talking about the poets and writers whose works he loved.

Occasionally, he would mention his family, but only some casual remark about recent happenings. Though I longed to ask him about the mystery which seemed to surround myself and the Courtneys, I dare not broach the subject directly, and though I was sometimes able to turn the conversation towards the Courtney ancestry, never, unfortunately, did Sir Hugh let slip any remark which would throw light upon the matter for me.

It was when the weather began to turn considerably colder towards the beginning of November that I first noticed a marked change in Sir Hugh's health. His hands began to shake and his speech was sometimes slurred. No other member of the family seemed to notice this and I said nothing as I told myself it was probably merely a sign of his age and not of ill health.

But on entering his study one November morning to ask him if he cared to come with me on a brisk walk to the river, I found him grasping the arm of his chair, his face purple, his breathing a rasping sound dragged painfully through his parted lips.

Frightened though I was, I managed to loosen his collar and to get him to lay back in his chair whilst I ran for help.

Fortunately, Bassett was just entering the hall as I flew out of his father's study.

'Bassett, come quickly. Your father is ill.'

He hurried towards me, alarm showing plainly on his face and we entered the study together.

'Fetch Jonathan and Charles, if he's at home,' said Bassett.

Quickly I ran in search of Jonathan, Sir Hugh's personal manservant, and having explained to him, I again ran on, through the corridors, up the wide stairs and along to the east wing.

Georgiana answered my impatient knock.

'Is Charles at home?' I said breathlessly.

'Yes, but...'

'Ask him to come quickly, it's your father, Georgiana, he's ill.'

'Charles,' Georgiana ran to her husband and he rose immediately from the desk where he was writing and took her hands.

'What is it, dearest?'

'It's my father. Louella says he is ill.'

Without hesitate, Charles ran the way I had come whilst Georgiana and I hastened after him, pausing only whilst she questioned me.

'Is he—very bad, Louella?' and her lower lip trembled.

'I didn't stay to see. I must be honest I made him as comfortable as I could then I ran to find—someone.'

I hesitated as I said the last word, for it suddenly struck me that when I had hurried from Sir Hugh's side in search of help, there had been one person on my mind—Bassett.

Even though I feared him, I acknowledged to myself that it was to him I knew I could run in trouble and in him find strength and help.

When we reached the hall, Charles and

Bassett were helping Sir Hugh to his bedroom.

Old Jonathan hovered anxiously behind his master.

Sir Hugh looked a little better than when I had first found him, but still he could not walk without assistance.

Later, comfortably settled in bed, Sir Hugh seemed much better, so Charles told us when he came in to the drawing-room, where we were all waiting for him.

Lady Courtney, who had now been told about her husband's illness, was the first to voice what was uppermost in all our minds.

'Have you any idea what it is?'

'As far as I can tell after a preliminary examination, it seem Sir Hugh has had a heart attack.'

Lady Courtney gasped.

'Serious?' asked Bassett.

'Not this one, but I'm afraid there may be more, each successively more serious and then, I am afraid...'

Charles did not need to finish for we all knew the full meaning behind his words.

Georgiana began to cry quietly and Charles crossed the room to comfort her.

'I'm sorry, my dear, perhaps I should not have told you.'

But Georgiana shook her head.

'No, Charles. I'd rather know.'

'Is there anything we can do?' said Lady Courtney. 'Bassett, should we call in a heart specialist?'

Bassett looked enquiringly at Charles.

'Don't think we underestimate your capabilities, Charles, but do you think?...'

'Of course, Bassett, you must do whatever you wish. Perhaps it would be as well since I am so closely connected if Sir Hugh were to be attended by another physician.' His arm went about Georgiana. 'In fact, I'd prefer it. Sir Joshua Fotheringhay is one of the best authorities I know on heart ailments. He lives but fifty miles from here. I'll set out immediately to fetch him.'

'No—no,' said Bassett, 'it's good of you, but it would be better if you stayed here.'

He thought quickly.

'One of my men from the village will go willingly, I am sure.'

'Then I will write an explanatory letter to him,' said Charles.

'That's a good idea.'

And they left the room together.

I turned to see Lady Courtney glaring at me.

'See what trouble you have brought upon us by your deception?'

For a moment I could not understand. Then I realised she was blaming the disappearance of the Courtney dagger for Sir Hugh's illness. And, of course, as she believed I had stolen it, I was the cause.

Bassett returned at that moment and so she said no more.

Sir Joshua arrived the next day, but he merely confirmed Charles' diagnosis.

He had an important medical conference to attend and could stay no longer than a few hours. Even the Courtney wealth could not buy the attention of this eminent main, whose devotion to the medical profession, would surely go down in history.

'There is little point in my staying, Mr Courtney. Your brother-in-law, Dr Corby, is a most capable young man. And I am afraid there is little I can do in Sir Hugh's case.'

The grey haired man shook his head sadly.

'I'm very sorry.' He cleared his throat

and added briskly, 'I've given Dr Corby detailed instructions as to exactly what may be done in any event. I'll come again in four days.'

'Thank you, Sir Joshua, it was good of you to come so quickly,' Bassett replied.

'Not at all, I only wish there was more I could do.'

So it was that the great physician left an unhappy household. There was little we could do and each day Sir Hugh sank lower. He had three more quite severe attacks and eventually, he would lapse into unconsciousness.

When he roused again he would become restless and fretful and would shout and ramble incessantly about his past life, his wife and my mother and other names, including his parents.

Early on the fourth morning after Sir Hugh had first been taken ill, I was awakened by a soft knock on my bedroom door. The pale light of dawn was only just beginning to glimmer through the curtains as I opened the door to find Bassett, his face tired and strained, his hair rumpled, standing there.

'Louella, I'm sorry to wake you. But father is in a very distressed state calling for Victoria.' He paused and said softly, 'I think perhaps if you would come, it might calm him.'

'Of course, Bassett, I'll come at once.'

I fetched my wrap and followed Bassett along the dimly lit corridor. Since Sir Hugh's illness, the corridor candles were kept burning throughout the night.

As I entered the sick-room, I was shocked to see the change in Sir Hugh. I had been to visit him several times during his illness, but mostly I had found him asleep. Now, for the first time, I was to see him threshing about the bed—his face shrunken and lined with suffering, his eyes wide and staring, and his brow wet with fever.

I took his hot hand in mine and spoke softly, and, I hope, soothingly.

Miraculously, it seemed to me, he began to quieten.

'Victoria,' he whispered, 'what are you doing here?'

'I've come to help you get well again.'

'Mama will not like you coming here—does she know?'

How could I answer him—I could not understand the meaning of his words. I looked enquiringly at Bassett.

He shook his head as if to tell me to reply negatively.

'No,' I told Sir Hugh, 'she doesn't know, and she won't find out. Now you lie quietly and try to sleep. You mustn't distress yourself so.'

Sir Hugh's pale lips parted in an effort to smile.

'Dear Victoria, your word is my command, always.'

And he slept.

I sighed with relief.

'Thank you, Louella. Jonathan and I have been trying for a long time to quieten him,' Bassett said, 'and to think you can do it so easily.'

'I'll stay with him as long as you wish me to, Bassett, you know that.'

'Thank you, my...' he stoped and ran his hand through his hair, his eyes dark with weariness.

'You must rest, Bassett. I'll stay with him now.'

'Very well. Perhaps I will, if you're sure?...'

'Of course.'

After Bassett and Jonathan had left, I sat in the still room and held Sir Hugh's hand as he slept and watched him. His face was now peaceful, no longer ravaged by distressing emotions. But I noticed that he had aged considerably since the start of his illness.

As I watched, pitying the sick man, his eyes flickered open and for a while he lay staring at the ceiling. I did not move or speak for I had no wish to disturb him. I prepared myself for further delirium. But he turned his head slowly on the pillow, the morning light catching his silver hair. He saw me and smiled.

'Ah, Louella, I am glad it is you with me. I wish to tell you something.'

I patted his hand comfortingly.

'You must not tire yourself, Sir Hugh. Try to rest. Whatever you have to tell me will wait.'

'No,' he whispered gently, 'I can wait no longer, my child, or I may leave it too late.'

The reference to his death was not made with self-pity but with resignation and peaceful acceptance. He was ready for death, ready for the release, but first he had something to tell me and I knew what it was.

He was, at last, going to tell me the secret surrounding my mother and me.

It was strange that now, as he neared death, for he undoubtedly did, his mind had cleared and he spoke slowly and deliberately, missing nothing in his tragic tale.

'Louella, my dear, before I begin, just reach into the drawer of that little table, here at my bedside. There is something I must return to you.'

I opened the drawer and there lay the missing miniature of my mother. Wordlessly, I picked it up and stood it on the table. Sir Hugh turned his head and looked at it for a long time. With a sigh he turned away again and began his story.

'Louella, many years ago, when I was a young man of twenty, we, the Courtneys, lived in this house, as we do now. My father was a weak-willed man who cared nothing for the fortunes amassed by his ancestors, and would undoubtedly have frittered it away leaving us penniless had it not been for my mother. She, Lady Florence Cunningham, had married my father in his heyday, before he had slipped into bad ways. She was a strong-minded, steadfast woman, an ardent believer in family tradition. She undertook to save the Courtney name and fortune as if it were her own family name. My brother and I were a constant disappointment to her. We lacked her vigour, her strength of character, and resembled more the weakness of my father. It was at this time that the Courtney dagger was sold by my father and its loss was blamed as the cause of the unhappy story I have to tell you.'

He paused, lost in memories, no doubt. I waited impatiently, but did not hurry him.

'There lived in Courtney village, the Lloyd family, a respectable family enough, well-born and well-bred, but poor. They were not of the aristocracy that my mother regarded the Courtneys were.

'Victoria and Virginia Lloyd were the beautiful daughters of the Lloyd household and one glorious summer, my brother James and I met the Lloyd sisters high on the hills surrounding Courtney estate. That summer was the only really happy time I remember in my life. We fell in love with the Lloyd girls, passionately, reverently and for ever.'

I saw the tears well in Sir Hugh's eyes, he was indeed reliving his happiness, and sadness, in telling me.

'I hardly need tell you the rest, Louella, do I? I fell in love with Victoria and James with Virginia, whom he later married.

'But being the eldest son and heir to the Courtney fortune I was expected to marry the woman of my parent's choice. She was Emily Bassett, daughter of Major Phillip Bassett and his wife, Georgiana, a family of equal standing to the Courtneys. I refused because I could never love her, not now that I had met the only woman I could ever love, Victoria. Even at twenty, I knew with one of those rare moments of wisdom in the young that Victoria was my one true love.

'It has been my life's regret, my remorse and shame that I was not strong enough to win the furious and bitter battle which ensued between my mother and myself over Victoria and Emily.

'James, of course, though my mother did her utmost to dissuade him, eventually married Virginia, for he was only the second son, and carried no family tradition to matter. My mother was heartless and remorseless in her refusal to allow my marriage to your mother. Had I been stronger, of her mettle, I would have spurned the family and married the woman I loved. For, Louella, I was a fortunate fellow in that your mother was gracious enough to love me. I use the word "gracious" purposely, for that is how I think of her as a woman, a lady, who in her spirit, in her character was worth far more than the Courtney name. She was her own individual gentility.'

He paused, for his long story was tiring, but he continued purposefully.

'But I gave way to my mother and married Emily Bassett. Poor Emily,' he spoke with pity, 'I have not made her happy, it has not been within my power when my heart belonged to another.

'Your mother left Courtney village, broken hearted, I believe, and four years later, she married a distant cousin of hers of the same name, Adam Lloyd. I met him only once some years before when he had visited the Lloyd family in Courtney. He, like me, loved her deeply.'

A gentle smile crossed Sir Hugh's weary face and much of the age slipped away.

'In fact, I cannot understand any man not loving her. Adam was good and kind to her but I believed she only loved him as second best, and for that I pitied him.

'I kept in touch, you understand, through James and Virginia, though I never saw my love again after that summer when we had met, fallen in love and parted, broken in spirit. Seven years after their marriage, you were born. But in giving you life, my child, your mother gave hers.'

He patted my hand comfortingly.

'I hope you never feel guilty about being the cause of your mother's death, for she would have had it no other way, my child, believe me. Your father, poor man, died a year later, broken and dispirited. He pined to death, they said. I could understand it, for I myself, at the news of Victoria's death, sank into a dark and dreadful time. Poor Emily, knowing from the beginning of my love for Victoria, could do nothing to pull me from my depression, and I believe if it had not been for my joy in my own two children, I should have allowed my life to drift away as Adam did. You were, as you know, cared for by Virginia and James, and they loved you as their own daughter.

'As you grew older it was obvious you would be the living image of your mother.

You brought joy and pain mingled to those around you for it was like having Victoria back with us again. Whenever you came to Courtney Hall as a child it was to revive sad memories for me and bitter thoughts for Emily.

'When Virginia died there was only James left belonging to you. And as you grew older it was impossible for a beautiful woman like you to remain alone with James Courtney. Tongues began to wag and to remember the old days, for, believe me, such scandals amongst the aristocracy are remembered and talked about for many, many years.

'So, poor child, you were brought to Courtney Hall, and I know you have suffered exceedingly at the hand of my wife and of Millicent.'

He turned and lifted himself on his pillows to clasp my hands in his.

'Dear little Louella, so like Victoria, I grieve to think of the pain I myself have caused you in my foolish ramblings in mistaking you for your mother. Now do you understand why Emily has hated and feared you?'

I nodded, unable to speak, for I pitied Emily Bassett Courtney for her years of unhappiness and at last I understood with compassion the reason for her hatred of me.

'Emily knew I have never been able to give her the love she had a right to. I doubt she has loved me for she has never shown it. Her love has been lavished on Bassett and her fierce protection and pride in him has perhaps compensated for the lack of love in her marriage. I hope so. I dearly hope so, for she did not deserve such a life. It was none of her doing.'

And Sir Hugh fell back on his pillow.

'There is just one more thing, child. I am sorry for taking your picture, but when I saw it in your room one day, the joy at having a likeness of your mother was too great to bear. I have drawn strength and comfort from it. Forgive me, child. Take it back for it is yours.'

'Keep it Sir Hugh, please, if it gives you happiness.'

'Bless you child, you do your mother proud. I will keep it only until I die, which will surely not be long, and then you must take it back.'

And without warning Sir Hugh lost consciousness once more.

He never regained it.

For two days and nights he lingered between the realms of life and the river of oblivion.

I insisted that I should attend to his wants personally.

Lady Courtney overcome with remorse and grief, now the end was near, gave way to hysteria and took to her bed.

Georgiana looked tired and strained with trying to comfort her mother and with the genuine grief that her gentle, absent-minded father would soon no longer pore over the yellowing pages of his beloved books. No longer would the small book-lined room he called his study be filled with his tobacco smoke, a warm refuge from the realities which faced him beyond its door.

Bassett commanded that I should rest, but I found sleep, restful sleep, impossible. I was disturbed by dreaming of Sir Hugh and my mother as young lovers, but their faces would change into Bassett and myself and then we would start quarrelling and I would wake feeling miserable.

Sir Hugh died peacefully. I was thankful that Bassett was with me. It was gone midnight and Bassett was insisting, in whispers, that I should retire. He said he would stay with his father until dawn when Charles would take over.

But our attention was drawn by the frail figure in the bed.

His breath was becoming laboured. His hands moved restlessly for a few moments and then—he was gone and his face at once became peaceful and serene. The years slipped away and he was almost a young man.

I saw the face my mother had loved. I saw in it the gentleness and kindness that, in its weakness, had been the cause of so much unhappiness.

Bassett stood by the bed looking down at his father.

Stirred by compassion for him, I moved to his side and instinctively sought and held his hand.

In that moment he was not the man I feared, but a son grief-stricken at his father's death, and whom I wanted to comfort.

His hand gripped mine. Then suddenly his arm was around my shoulders and he was leading me from the room.

Together we went down the dimly lit stairs past the flickering candles.

In the hall old Jonathan waited anxiously, knowing there was trouble.

'It's the end, Jonathan,' Bassett's voice was strong but a tone deeper with the emotion he held in check. 'See to everything, will you?'

The old man's eyes filled with tears and his aged back seemed to bend even more as his master left the Earth.

'Of course. I'm very sorry, Sir Bassett.'

Bassett stiffened and I stared at the unfamiliar use of Bassett's hereditary title.

Bassett turned towards his father's study and opened the door. We moved into the dark room. A fire still burned brightly in the grate and Sir Hugh's faithful hound, Juniper, raised sorrowful eyes to us and whined pitifully and knowingly.

Bassett stroked the dog's head soothingly and sat down in his father's old leather chair.

The firelight flickered, a log fell and sparks flew throwing strange shadows on the wall.

I knelt on the rug before the fire at Bassett's feet.

I forgot my dislike of him, I forgot his cold treatment of me during the past months. I forgot even that he was my husband. In that small room, Bassett, now Sir Bassett Courtney, truly Master of Courtney, was just a young man grieving for his father, a man I wanted to comfort.

He bent forward, gazing into the fire, his elbows resting on his knees, his hands clasped together.

Overcome by a feeling of tenderness aroused by the look of sadness on his face, I took his strong hands in mine and laid my cheek against them.

He did not spurn my action and we sat for a long time saying nothing. Then, as if to relieve the pain he felt that his father would no longer sit in that very chair, would no longer amble through the great corridors of Courtney Hall, would no longer call me Victoria, Basset began to talk about Sir Hugh.

'Poor father, he had such little happiness in his life. He may have seemed to you a weak insignificant man.'

'No, Bassett, never. He was a gentle person who only wished to live in peaceful harmony.'

'He never enjoyed the life of stress and strain attached to amassing the Courtney fortune,' and once more Bassett's tone was bitter as he spoke of his family's wealth.

'He's been happier since he handed that over to me.'

He paused and his voice was full of sadness.

'But I knew he was always there if I needed his advice. And now he won't be there any more.'

What could I say in comfort? I grieved for my own part at the loss of Sir Hugh, who had recently become my friend. And now that I had heard the full story surrounding himself and my mother, I felt even more love for him because he had loved my mother and had also been loved by her in return.

'Sir Hugh told me about my mother,' I told Bassett softly.

'Did he? I'm glad. I thought you should have known long ago, but it was not my secret to reveal.'

'That's just what Georgiana said once.'

There was a moment's silence then I said,

'Poor Lady Courtney hasn't had a happy life either knowing about it all.'

Bassett smiled, though the sadness remained in his eyes.

'Even though she has been so cruel to you, you can still find pity for her?

I looked up into those deep brown eyes of his.

'I understand now what my coming here must have meant for her, for you all. No doubt I would have done much the same in her position.'

'I think not,' Bassett said softly, 'but I am thankful and grateful that you can forgive.'

We sat in silence in the firelight for some time, neither of us wanting to leave the safety of this cosy room. Neither wanted to face the reality beyond the door. Death, mourning and all the necessary arrangements which Bassett would have to make.

The funeral was a lavish affair. I had never seen such grandeur bestowed upon what was after all now a lifeless and useless body. It seemed to me that it would have been far kinder if all the people who arrived clad in black, the women who pressed handkerchiefs to their lips and dabbed their tearful eyes, had given Sir Hugh more affection and attention during his life, there would have been far more sense in it. Lady Courtney, now composed from her brief bout of what I

215

supposed was genuine grief, now retained a stony expression and there was no trace of tears in her eyes.

The slow funeral procession seemed never-ending as it wound down the hill from Courtney Hall and to the small church, where only weeks before all the people who now followed in mournful guise, had attended Bassett's wedding, for them a joyful occasion.

The whole village, I am sure, without exception, fell into step behind the family mourners and their tears were at least genuine sorrow. The solemn service soon over, the coffin was lowered into the cold earth. Sir Hugh's grave had been placed next to his parents and beside his were further vacant plots for the rest of the Courtney family. I shuddered. This was a sorrowful place, and I knew Sir Hugh would have hated it as much as I did.

And so the funeral party returned to the Hall, Sir Bassett, and I, now Lady Courtney, how strange the title seemed, leading the way.

Poor Sir Hugh was gone, and now his son was truly Master of Courtney Hall. And as I watched his face, still showing traces of the natural grief he felt,

I seemed to see it grow older and take on an even sterner expression now that he had complete control of the Courtney wealth.

CHAPTER NINE

The days passed quickly enough, for after the funeral, there were vast changes to be made as regards our living quarters. Those we had recently inhabited since our marriage were now vacated in favour of the main part of the Hall. Lady Courtney, now as the dowager Lady Courtney, so to speak, moved into the west wing which had been the home of Bassett and myself for such a short time.

'You will have to take on more of the management of the house now, Louella. I shall insist upon it, even though mother may resist, for I think you should learn the running of this house as soon as possible.'

I felt he was implying that I had much to learn and perhaps he was justified in thinking this, for I had not much idea where to begin or what was expected of me.

'You'll also have to accompany me on business trips. I know this is perhaps unusual, women are expected to stay at home. But the trend seems to be that a woman should take more part in her husband's affairs and I intend to see that you do.'

'Yes, Bassett,' I said meekly with far more acquiescence in my tone than I felt, for inwardly I was seething with indignation. But what was the point in showing this feeling? I knew from the past where it would lead me.

So, by degrees, with the patient and understanding help of Georgiana, Jonathan and the kitchen staff, I began to take over the reins as mistress of Courtney Hall. Needless to say, I received no help at all from Lady Courtney, but at least times were a little happier for I saw a good deal less of her than previously.

Millicent returned to the Hall, after a short absence. My newly acquired confidence in managing the household affairs suffered a sharp blow for her vicious tongue never let me forget who I was, nor how I had usurped her rightful position.

Christmas was upon us in no time and Bassett decided that though the Courtney family must, out of customary respect, have only a quiet festival, there was no reason why the villagers should suffer.

'It's always been the custom, Louella,' he told me on one of the many sessions I now had to have in his study, receiving instructions as to what he required me to do. 'That the Courtneys give a ball for the villagers to attend on New Year's Eve. Usually we hold our own banquet and ball on Boxing Day for all our family and guests, to which none of the villagers are invited. But on New Year's Eve we provide the ballroom, the food and leave them to enjoy themselves. The Master of Courtney makes a customary appearance at midnight, but otherwise it is their evening to enjoy in their own way with none of the Courtneys present.'

'And you want this ball for the villagers still to take place?' I asked.

'Yes. I have spoken to one or two of the villagers and though they feel perhaps they ought to join us in our period of mourning, I think that they would feel somewhat disappointed if thwarted of their usual revelry. So we shall still hold that one, but not our own.'

The next weeks therefore, preceding Christmas were for me not only extremely busy, but agonising with all the responsibility of making this banquet a success. Bassett left the entire arrangements to me, and had it not been for Georgiana's support and advice, no doubt the villages would still be waiting for their evening's pleasure.

As it was, I managed fairly well and the evening of the ball found me standing in the middle of the vast ballroom surveying the result of my efforts. All the weeks of ordering decorations, flowers, masses of food, an orchestra, all culminated in the result before my eyes.

Bright tinsel hung from every part of the room, shimmering in the soft light of thousands of candles—for what was more romantic than candlelight? A traditional Christmas tree stood in the corner, its topmost point almost touching the ceiling. From every branch there swung a gift for every member of the village. Bassett had said no expense was to be spared, and though I had sometimes wondered at my extravagance, Georgiana assured me that I was spending no more money than usual.

'Bassett, more than any of his predecessors, yes, even poor, dear father, likes to give his tenants pleasure and reward for their loyalty,' she told me.

Indeed he does, I thought to myself now as I viewed the result. Above my head hung a huge bunch of mistletoe and as I looked up at it, I visualised many a courtship being sealed beneath it tonight, and maybe several new beginnings.

'Wishful thinking, Louella?' a deep voice said behind me, and I swung round startled to see Bassett a few feet from me.

How foolish I felt, so I said crossly,

'Of course not. Who would want to meet me beneath the mistletoe?'

Bassett smiled that sarcastic smile of his.

'Why me, of course,' and with swift steps he reached me.

Bassett swept me to him. I was powerless against his strength although I pushed against his chest.

For a moment his dark eyes gazed mockingly into mine. Then he bent his head and kissed me hard—so hard that my mouth was bruised.

I was startled and angry at the thrill of excitement which stirred within me. And my anger sought revenge.

I opened my mouth very slightly so that his lip forced its way between my teeth. Then, like any savage dog, I bit sharply. Bassett sprang away and clapped his hand to his mouth but not before I saw that I had drawn blood. His face was dark with anger.

'You little vixen,' he mumbled, his voice shaking.

Suddenly, he roared with laughter, his tones ringing through the great ballroom.

'The girl has spirit, but I'll tame you yet,' his voice softened, and an almost gentle expression crossed his face.

'Yes, little Louella, I'll tame you yet,' and he strode from the room.

I tried to smile to myself, to feel some satisfaction, but I was surprised at the realisation that I was neither angry now, nor pleased with what I had done. I was ashamed I had behaved in such a manner. Bassett had every right to kiss me, I told myself, my cheeks flaming. It was only because he was a gentleman that he forced no further attentions on me, coupled with the fact, of course, that he did not love me.

And above my head the mistletoe swung in mockery.

The ball was a huge success and greatly enjoyed by all the villagers. Bassett told me afterwards that when he went there at midnight, many of the villagers in making their thanks to him, had complimented me on my organisation and said it was quite the best they had ever attended. This pleased Bassett and he seemed to have forgotten the affair of the kiss under the mistletoe. My womanly pride suffered a blow for obviously the kiss had meant nothing to him from the start, but I had tried, by repelling him so viciously, to turn it into something he had never intended.

I was glad, however, that the villagers had enjoyed themselves, for little did I realise when I worked so hard at the preparations that they were to have little enjoyment for a long time after that night. Indeed, they were about to enter a time of severe hardship and misery. On the following morning, on the very first day of the New Year, the snows began.

At first, the snow seemed harmless enough, beautifying the countryside with its layer of virgin white. But day after day the snow continued to fall, until the whole surrounding land was enveloped in deep drifts. Many sheep were lost on the hillsides, and the men of the village fought their way through miles of snow in the hope of finding them.

Bassett soon shed any superiority as Master of Courtney and joined his men in the battle against the weather. Night after night, day after day, he worked side by side with his men. And they loved him for it.

This, then, was what the old men of the village had foretold in their warnings of flooding, for it soon became apparent to everyone that when a thaw set in, the hillside streams and the river itself would never cope with the vast deluge of water.

Preliminary steps were taken for the villagers to salvage as much as possible from their homes and the outbuildings at Courtney Hall, fortunately there were many, soon became crammed with the belongings of the villagers.

The threat of flooding hung over us for weeks, but it was not until the beginning of February that I knew the fear would become a reality. The snow stopped falling and with it came a spell of milder weather. The snow on the hills began to melt rapidly, aggravated by a wind which sprang up and reached gale force. It blew the remaining snow into drifts, and drove the water of the streams surging down into the valley to wreck the villagers' homes.

I was coming down the wide main staircase when the huge door was flung wide. The gale, which had been raging all night, filled the hall, rippling the carpet and billowing the heavy curtains. As if part of the rushing wind, Bassett forged into the hall. Catching sight of me, he stopped and hesitated. He swept back his windblown hair impatiently with his hand.

His stern expression was even more serious, almost desperate, than I had thought possible.

Sir Bassett Courtney was a worried man.

Forgetting everything but the fact that something was obviously very wrong, I picked up my skirts and ran down the remaining few steps.

'Bassett,' I cried, 'what is wrong?'

'The river, Louella, the river has burst its banks—as we feared.'

'Oh, Bassett, how dreadful. Has it reached the houses yet?'

'No, thank God, but it won't be long.'

He sat down in the heavy, carved oak chair and leant back wearily.

We looked at each other and both thought the same thing.

The tentative plans we had made for sheltering the homeless villagers must be put into action and quickly.

I tried to smile comfortingly, but now I was worried too. There was suffering and danger ahead for the Courtneys and their people.

And I knew who would get the blame.

I, who was believed to have stolen the Courtney dagger, would be held responsible by several for having brought disaster once more upon the Courtneys.

But there was nothing I could do. I could not undo something I had never done.

At that moment Lady Courtney followed by Millicent, Georgiana and even Evelyn who had recently come up from the village to stay at Courtney Hall because of the danger of flooding to her home, joined us in the hall.

Bassett turned to face them as he rose. 'The river has bursts its banks. I'm sending most of the village folk whose homes are threatened up here. They'll stay here until their homes are safe for them to return.'

Lady Courtney's eyes held disapproval, Georgiana's anxiety, but the look which passed between Millicent and Evelyn puzzled me the most. They looked really frightened.

'Bassett, is this really necessary?' Lady Courtney was saying. 'All those dreadful people trampling round our home.'

'Yes, it is necessary,' Bassett said curtly and his eyes met his mother's in determination.

Lady Courtney shrugged and turned away.

'As you wish. 'Tis no more than I expected since we are now destined to misfortune and degradation since the theft of the dagger.'

The others followed her to the drawing-room and Bassett and I were alone again.

I could see Bassett was angry with his mother for her lack of compassion for the homeless villagers.

He turned to me. Taking me gently by the shoulders, he looked me straight in the eyes.

'Louella, take care of the villagers for me.' His voice hardened. 'Mother is useless in a crisis like this.'

'Yes, Bassett, I will. Don't worry, we'll

see they have all they need.'

He smiled, but the worry never left his eyes. He brushed my forehead with his lips.

'Thank you, dearest,' he murmured, and before I could be sure of what he said, he had gone from the house and away down to the village to send the people up to Courtney Hall.

I went in search of Mary and Jonathan. There was a great deal we had to do to prepare food and beds for our guests.

Cook, bless her kind heart, was a marvel at making what provisions she had go a long way. She at once began to bake and cook, and soon trays of pastries, cakes and bowls of warm soup and the like were covering all parts of her vast kitchen.

Mary and I began to arrange the sleeping quarters. We decided to put the women and young children in the ballroom, and the men and older boys in the dining-room and library. The older folk would be given the bedrooms as far as possible with more comfort. Most of the villagers would be told to bring as much bedding as possible, for we had no spares other than the spare beds.

Soon the first families began to arrive

and I went to the hall to greet them and to try to make them sure of their welcome.

Lady Courtney had disappeared. I expected she meant to stay out of the way, but I had no time to worry about her feelings.

Mrs Cartwright and her four children and Mrs Wain and her two came first.

'Ever so good of the master, it is, ma'am, to 'ave us. But then, you's kind folk.'

I took some of the heavy load of blankets and led the way.

'Think nothing of it, Mrs Cartwright,' I told her from behind an armful of blankets. 'We can't possibly leave you all down there in the village.'

We entered the ballroom, now transformed from the awe-inspiring grandeur of shimmering chandeliers and cold marble floors, to a warm inviting dormitory. Welcoming fires burnt in three huge grates down one side of the room and on the other the thick brocade curtains had been drawn across the long windows shutting out the wild, fearsome weather.

Mrs Cartwright was soon followed by more of her fellow villagers. Young and old alike—calm and resigned to whatever

Fate held for them, grateful for the shelter we offered them.

The old people were almost too awe-struck to enter the luxurious bedrooms and each vowed they would not dare to sleep on the bed.

Comforting them, supplying them with food, cradling whimpering babies, I was soon very tired and thankful at last to return to my own bedroom and fling myself on the bed.

But I could not rest long, for Mary soon fetched me to go to little Albert Whittaker, a baby of ten months, whose mother, a young girl of twenty, was beside herself with worry over him.

The child was running a high fever and I knew Charles was the only person who could help us.

'Stay with Mrs Whittaker, Mary. I'll fetch Dr Corby.'

'I've just seen him with old Tom in the Blue Room, madam,' Mary said.

But when I reached the bedroom I found old Tom alone, peacefully dozing in a chair by the fire.

Hurriedly, I ran in search of Charles. He was not in his own rooms in the east wing. I approached the main stairs and heard his voice in the hall below. I was about to call out to him, when I realised he was talking to Evelyn. So instead I went down the stairs and in so doing could not help but hear their conversation.

'Charles,' Evelyn was saying, 'I must go home. There is something I must fetch.'

Her eyes were wide with fear.

Charles gripped her shoulders almost cruelly.

'Don't be so foolish, Evelyn. The house may be swept away any moment. It is already flooded. How do you expect to get there?'

'I don't know. I don't know,' she answered wildly, 'but I must go—I must.'

'Why?'

'I—can't tell you.'

'I'll go, if it is so important,' he sighed. 'What is it you want fetching?'

Evelyn's glance dropped to the floor and she turned away as Charles loosened his grip.

'No,' she whispered, clearly still distressed. 'It's not that important. You must not go.'

And she left the hall.

Charles ran his hands through his hair.

'Whatever has got into her? I've never seen her like this.'

'Charles,' I said urgently, 'I'm sorry to interrupt, but young Mabel Whittaker's baby, Albert, seems very ill—can you come and look at him?'

Charles' love and concern for his patients pushed all thoughts of family problems aside immediately and he followed me swiftly to the child.

Albert's eyes were large, dark circles in his hot little face. He lay on the bed wrapped in a shawl, his breathing a rasping, painful sound. He was quiet, but his eyes, even though so young, showed fear and pain.

Charles was gentle and examined the child with the minimum of fuss.

'Pneumonia,' he said softly to me. 'Don't alarm the mother—we must do all we can.'

The next few hours were a turmoil of following Charles' instructions in nursing the sick baby. Charles persuaded the distraught mother to rest and leave the care of her child to us. Her trust in Dr Corby was implicit and soon she was asleep in the next room. But there was no rest for Charles or me that night. He said the fever would reach a climax around two o'clock in the morning.

I hardly remember what we did except watch and wait and be there to ease the poor mite's breathing as best we could.

Bassett arrived home about midnight and Georgiana, still helping the villagers settle for the night, told him of our vigil. He came to the bedroom where we watched over little Albert.

He stood for a long time looking down at the baby whose tiny finger clasped mine tightly.

'Will he be all right, Charles?' he asked softly.

Charles, his fair hair ruffled, his brow wet in the heat of the room which was necessary for the child in such a fever, replied,

'We shall know by two in the morning, if not before.'

Bassett nodded.

'I'll look in again then.'

I thought he seemed about to speak to mc and I looked up at him. His face was in shadow from the low light on the table, so I could not see him clearly—just the clear-cut outline of his firm jaw, the wide brow and arrogant nose.

But he said no more and went quietly from the room and I turned my attention back to little Albert.

Charles and I did not speak much. We were both tired, and all our efforts were concentrated upon caring for the child.

The minutes dragged, but two o'clock came at last and passed.

About half-an-hour later than Charles had anticipated the baby's fever broke and we passed the crisis safely. We both heaved a thankful prayer of relief and though no doubt Charles was used to such efforts as a doctor, for me it was the first time I had helped to save a life, for Charles said we had certainly done just that between us.

A little later Bassett returned, still fully clothed, and I knew he was too worried and restless to sleep.

'There is no more Louella can do,' Charles said to Bassett. 'I'll stay with the child. See she gets some rest, Bassett.'

Now that the crisis was over, the exhaustion seemed to sweep over me and I could hardly find the strength to walk to my room. Bassett, his arm round me, helped from the room, leaving Charles still sitting by the child's bedside.

I stumbled along beside him and

suddenly felt his strong arms lift me and carry me the rest of the way to my room. I remembered him laying me gently on the bed and then I knew no more as I fell into a deep, exhausted sleep.

The next thing I knew was Georgiana tiptoeing through the door and smiling into my weary eyes late the next morning.

She placed a breakfast tray before me.

'Poor Louella,' she said, 'you seem to be bearing all the visitors' troubles.'

I sighed.

'How is Albert?'

'Still sleeping. Charles says he will pull through, but it was a close thing a few hours ago.'

I nibbled the toast, not really hungry—I was still too tired.

Georgiana sat on the bed and said, a little too casually.

'Did you see Evelyn last night? She's not in her room and her bed looks as though it's not been slept in.'

I looked up at her, startled.

'Only when I fetched Charles to the baby.'

'I don't want to worry Charles, just now, he's so tired,' Georgiana frowned, 'but I have the uneasy feeling she may have been stupid enough to try and go home—I know she wanted to.'

'Oh no,' I sat up quickly nearly spilling the tray, and grasped Georgiana's arm.

'Of course, now I remember. That's what she and Charles were arguing about when I fetched him. Go and tell Charles at once. She may be in danger.'

'But I don't know for certain she's gone.'

'Of course she has, if she's missing,' I said impatiently. 'She was so determined to go home.'

But Bassett was the one whose help Georgiana sought. She wanted, at first, to protect her husband from worry. Bassett set out immediately with two of the villagers to go to the Corbys' house to see if Evelyn was there, for a thorough search through Courtney Hall revealed that she had certainly disappeared somewhere.

But as they were gone a long time, Charles could be kept ignorant no longer. By this time I had risen and went with Georgiana to tell him.

Charles was very angry to think that Evelyn had not only disobeyed him, but had caused others to place themselves in danger by going to look for her.

'The foolish girl,' he said marching up and down. 'How could she? The house is already flooded—I told her.'

A cold fear began to spread through me. I could see that Charles feared for Evelyn's safety, but I, I realised with shock, feared for Bassett now that he had gone to that very house to look for her.

Georgiana too seemed to sense our mounting fear for she took Charles' hand and held out her other hand to me.

'Come,' she said firmly, 'we shall go to the front door to watch for their return.'

The howling wind tore at our clothes as we opened the huge door. Black clouds scudded overhead threatening more rain to add to the already overflowing river.

Bassett's horse rounded the sweep of the drive and he rode straight up to the front door. He had been gone some three hours in search of Evelyn and now he returned alone, without even the searchers who had gone with him.

I think we all knew he had grave news from the look on his face as he entered the hall. We waited, as Millicent and Lady Courtney joined us, to hear what he had to say.

'Charles,' Bassett's tone was deep. 'I

have bad news. Evelyn reached home, but was swept away on her return to the Hall. We have found her body—the villagers are bringing her here.'

Georgiana put her arms round her husband and tried to comfort him. He swallowed hard and nodded to Bassett.

'Thank you for going in search of her,' he said hoarsely.

'I fear there is more to tell you, Charles. I'm sorry, at such a time, but I must.'

Bassett took from beneath his mud-bespattered cloak a parcel of cloth.

He unfolded this blue cloth and there across the palm of his hand lay the shimmering Courtney dagger.

Bassett's voice was low and solemn and his eyes turned apologetically to Charles' stunned face.

'This was found beneath Evelyn's cloak, wrapped in this cloth. She was bringing it back to Courtney Hall.'

'Then...?' Charles dragged his eyes, mesmerised, from the dagger to meet Bassett's gaze. 'Then Evelyn—took it?' he whispered and added, with a trace of anger even through his grief, 'and let Louella take the blame?'

Before anyone could answer, a sob

escaped Millicent's lips and the stricken look on her face caught Bassett's, indeed everyone's attention.

'What is it, Millicent?' he said.

She flung herself forward and clung to Bassett's arm.

'Bassett, Bassett, forgive me. Had I known all this would happen...' and she began to weep uncontrollably.

'Did you have something to do with this, Millicent?' His tone was none too gentle, but his arm was about her shoulders.

She nodded miserably and her whisper was barely audible to the rest of us.

'I planned it—with Evelyn.'

'Why?' Bassett asked incredulously.

'Bassett,' her eyes looked up into his appealingly, 'need you ask?'

Suddenly, he became aware of us all watching and waiting.

'I think we had better discuss this in my study, Millicent.'

And with his arm still about her, they left us and disappeared.

No one knew what passed behind the closed door of Bassett's study, but Millicent appeared almost an hour later, dry-eyed but subdued and almost a changed person.

They joined us in the drawing-room.

Lady Courtney watched them enter and immediately Bassett's eyes met hers. The look which passed between them told me all I needed to know.

Lady Courtney, if not a prime mover in the theft of the dagger and the subsequent blame upon me, had not been entirely ignorant of the true facts, I was certain.

But Bassett evidently understood her motives, as, indeed, did I now, and from the expression in his eyes, I knew he pitied her.

But Lady Courtney pursed her lips and looked away, as if she despised his pity.

The matter was not referred to again except between Charles and me. The poor man, stricken with natural grief for the sister who had sacrificed so much to ensure his career, had the additional sadness of knowing that she had participated in the plot of theft which had overshadowed all our lives for so long.

'Louella, how can I ask your forgiveness?' he said to me on the day of Evelyn's funeral, as we, Georgiana, Charles and I, waited in the small sitting-room where he and Georgiana had found so much happiness, in their own suite of rooms.

'Charles, my dear, that is all past. Please

forget it, for all our sakes, not least your own. It was only because of her love for you, she dreaded losing you to anyone—to me as she thought.'

'You're so generous and good, Louella,' Georgiana said, taking my hand. 'Evelyn must have been so jealous of you, poor thing.'

'She never had a normal, happy life,' said Charles. 'Mother and father were so demanding. I escaped their clutches when I went to college, but poor Evelyn, by the time her release came at their death, had forgotten or never learned how to enjoy life. But how I wish she had never done this, and to you, Louella, of all people.'

'Please try to forget it,' I begged, 'and think of her only with affection. She is to be pitied, not blamed or despised.'

I must admit that it was because I was so relieved that the truth had been discovered and that I was proved blameless in Bassett's eyes, that I had no feeling of anger or peevishness against those who had wronged me. I merely wanted it to be forgotten.

'Very well, I'll try,' and Charles smiled a little. 'Come, it is time we went.'

The funeral, which took place only three

days after Evelyn's body had been found, was held amidst the gales and torrential rain which still buffeted and massacred our valley. Fortunately, the little church remained, like Courtney Hall, unscathed. How the funeral arrangements had been made, I do not know. How different it was from Sir Hugh's final farewell, when not a soul in the village had stayed away, when very few eyes were devoid of tears for the gentle man they had loved and whose son they adored.

Evelyn was laid to rest in a corner of the churchyard not far from the shadow of the proud Courtney tombstones.

Only Charles, Georgiana, Bassett and I attended the funeral as mourners, and as soon as we returned to the Hall from the church, we were plunged immediately back into the trouble which surrounded us all.

Bassett immediately changed his clothing and left the Hall to go out into the wild storm to look for more lost animals reported to be missing from the higher slopes.

Charles was soon called to attend to his patients. Several of the older folk were beginning to suffer from the shock and the young doctor was needed everywhere at once, it seemed. Georgiana and I were also finding it difficult to find enough food to feed all our guests. Supplies were dwindling fast, and with the road cut off out of the valley we could see no way of getting further supplies.

'When will it end, Louella?' she said miserably. 'Now the dagger is back, surely it must stop.'

'I fear the dagger has little to do with it,' I said, 'I only wish it had, for then we should be nearing the end of our troubles.'

Little did I know how right I was in my disbelief in the dagger's powers, for as the night closed in once more, bringing with it a worsening of the fearsome gale, Bassett had still not returned to the Hall.

CHAPTER TEN

All the men who had accompanied Bassett in search of stranded animals returned one by one before nightfall, saying that their master had instructed them to return to the Hall before darkness. He had gone on alone down to the valley to search the houses, those he could reach, for food.

With the tragedy of Evelyn's death still in our minds, we were all afraid for Bassett's safety. I tried to busy myself with work, but all too often I found myself peering into the wild darkness for some sign of his return.

And now, with the suddenness of a physical blow, I realised I loved Bassett. I was shaken as at last I admitted it to myself.

Never during all the unhappiness I had suffered recently, had I visited such utter depths of misery.

Bassett must be dead by this time, for it was almost eight hours since he had left the house shortly after four o'clock in the afternoon.

Too late I realised I loved him. Too late to tell him. Too late to try to erase the bitterness and hatred I had shown towards him. Here I was a virgin widow with no happy memories to console me, only a heart heavy with remorse and shame for my foolish pride.

The blessed relief of tears was denied me. I sat in my room, a solitary statue, gazing unseeingly from my window across the dark, flooded land, where I was sure, now, Bassett lay.

Unbidden thoughts from the past began to torture me: Bassett's warm smile when we first met: our first ride together before Millicent's arrival spoilt it: his belief in me at Georgiana's request when the dagger disappeared: his anger when I had argued with him over Georgiana's marriage to Cedric Rothbone and again when he met me returning from a moonlight meeting with Charles.

But my thoughts dwelt mainly on the times when he had smiled and laughed, when he had spoken directly to me, when the expression on his face had left me wondering. Whether he cared, if only a little, for me or not? Not until now had it mattered. But now, though it was too late, my mind searched back over the days and weeks remembering Bassett's every look, his tone of voice, searching in desperation for some sign of affection towards me.

With a sob I buried my head in my hands. I had to admit it, there had never been any time when I could say, with certainty, that he had shown any love for me. Even the times when his lips had brushed my brow in a gentle kiss, it held no more than brotherly affection. The only time he had kissed me with feeling, I had behaved so dreadfully and again shame swept over me at the memory.

I realised now that in all probability the reason why I had not made a serious attempt to escape marriage to Bassett was because I had loved him for some time, but my pride had blinded my reason.

But now my pride was swept away in humble grief and I acknowledged the truth.

The clock ticked away the minutes and one o'clock in the morning came and went with still no news. The rest of the family had now retired to their rooms. Though they were no doubt as distressed as I was, they evidently felt there was no more they could do.

A party of men from the village set off once more in the direction of the flooded houses to search for their master. I was impatient with them, for I felt they were searching in the wrong direction. Bassett was no fool. He would keep to the higher ground, attempting to gain access to those houses not badly affected by the rising water.

There was a soft knock upon my door,

the way Bassett knocked. I jumped up and ran to open it. But Jonathan stood there, alone. His back even more bent, his face solemn, and I thought I saw the trace of tears glistening in his old eyes.

'Madam, I thought you should know. The master's horse has returned home—riderless.'

I gasped and knew I turned white.

'Oh Jonathan, the master has not—he...?'

'No Madam. There is no word yet.'

'Thank you,' I whispered, as he turned away and left me. I realised what I must do. I must go in search of Bassett myself.

I changed quickly into my riding habit and moved silently and swiftly down the stairs, through the hall and out into the wild night. In the stables I chose the horse I had ridden on that first ride with Bassett. I was thankful that Uncle James had taught me not only to ride but also to saddle a horse and care for the animal.

I mounted and left the stable, the horse's hooves clopping on the stones. I feared the household may hear our departure. But the gale was so violent, that I felt sure no sound would be heard above its roaring.

The wind tore at my riding habit and snatched my breath away. The rain lashed about me, and stung my face and hands. But I must keep on for whilst there was breath in my body, I would search for Bassett, or until I knew for certain that he was dead. I shuddered at the word and prayed that it would not be so.

The horse, poor creature, was terrified of the storm, but I knew she would not throw me. She was a stout-hearted animal and though she was afraid, it would take a great deal to make her forget the safety of her rider.

The search party had gone down towards the village to look for Bassett at the water's edge. I believed he would not, level-headed as always, endanger himself more than necessary and would keep to the hills.

So I turned the horse in the opposite direction from the tumbling floods. The moon, at times hidden by scudding storm clouds, gave uncertain light. My cloak billowed from my body and if it had not been tied about my neck, it would doubtless have been tossed down the hillside.

I leant closer to the horse's neck as the gallant creature struggled on, her hooves slipping on the sodden turf. But gradually we gained ground. We passed streams gurgling down the hillside, rushing to join the already overladen river.

Had it ever rained so before? Had all this been caused by the theft of the dagger? But surely, now the dagger had been returned to the Courtneys, the storm should cease and everything should come right.

There was no sense, I told myself sharply, in pinning hope on an age-old superstition. For the storm still raged, Bassett was still missing and here was I, a pathetic, bedraggled girl, vainly searching for the man I loved.

A light glimmered ahead. It was old Tom's hut. Reason told me I should head for it and rest a while before continuing the search. But my heart wanted to drive me forward, looking unceasingly for Bassett.

The horse stumbled and whinnied in pain, almost throwing me.

So reason won. I would be helpless without the horse and no man would thank me for driving the creature beyond endurance.

Instinct kept the horse on a steady path towards the light, for exhausted with caring for the villagers, my distress over Bassett and now physically buffeted by the storm, I was beyond guiding the animal in any way. It was all I could do to remain on her back.

The light shone from the shepherd's hut. I slid from the saddle and fell towards the door. Feebly, I knocked. I leant against the door jamb and waited. I heard the scrape of a chair being pushed back and footsteps.

The latch lifted and the light from the lamp blinded me. I blinked up at the tall man in the doorway and heard his startled exclamation.

'Louella!'

'Bassett,' my voice was a hoarse whisper of thankfulness.

Bassett held out his arms and I fell into them weeping.

It was some time before I could speak, think or hear coherently. Bassett held me and stroked my hair until my sobs had quietened. As I drew back and looked up into his face, I saw him wince in pain. I looked down swiftly to see his shirt was torn and stained not only with mud but with blood.

'Bassett,' I cried, 'your arm. Is it hurt?'

'A little. It's nothing. Come and sit by the fire. You're soaked to the skin.'

'Let me see your arm—how bad is it?'

'You'll catch your death of cold.'

'I shall attend to your arm first,' I said firmly.

He was so tired that he ceased to argue. He sat down in front of the fire whilst I found some clean bandage and first aid equipment in a small cupboard which Tom used. I bathed his arm and dressed it.

As I rolled his sleeve down again, Bassett put his other arm about my waist as I stood over him.

'You were very brave to come and look for me, Louella.' He sighed and leant his head against me.

I looked down at his tousled dark hair, his clothes torn and stained, and my love for him flowed through me so strongly that I was sure he must feel it.

But before I betrayed my feelings for him, I must find out why he had married me.

'Bassett,' I said hesitantly. My fingers hovered above his ruffled hair—I longed to stroke it but dared not.

'Yes?'

'Why did you marry me?' His arm tightened about my waist but as he did not answer, I added, 'Was it to avoid marrying Millicent, as your mother wished?'

He looked up at me then.

'How could you think such a thing? You know that's not true. I'd never marry but for...' He looked away and sighed.

'...but for love,' he said softly. 'I suppose it was very wrong of me to force you to marry me when you despise me so. But I love you, Louella. I've loved you from the first moment I saw you peeping over the banisters that first day you arrived.'

Joy surged through me, I felt faint with happiness. But I checked myself and allowed him to finish.

'But the Courtney pride would not let me crawl to you, especially as the more I came to love you, the more you hated me. The times I've seemed so angry—when you returned from that meeting with Charles just before he eloped with Georgiana or when you refused to buy clothes for yourself—it was only because I loved you I was either consumed with jealousy or miserable because I loved in vain.

'On our wedding day when you would not look at me, it almost broke my heart and the night I stood and watched you with the baby, the way he held your fingers so trustingly, and you looking so beautiful, it was all I could do to stop myself from taking you in my arms there and then.

'I hoped, if we married, you might come to love me. I'm sorry.'

Bassett kept his eyes averted whilst he told me this and could not see my face, otherwise he could have seen my love for him written in my eyes.

I put my arms about him and pressed my cheek to his hair.

'But I do love you,' I whispered.

Slowly, as if unable to believe the words, he rose and took me in his arms.

'Say that again,' and as I did his eyes shone with a happiness I had never seen light the eyes of the master of Courtney Hall before.

And in that small hut away upon the hillside, I, drenched and bedraggled, and Bassett, his clothes torn, his arm hurt, we found the happiness for which we had both searched for so long.

And as if rejoicing in our happiness and love, the gale began to lessen and as dawn broke, a pale though watery sun, greeted us.

We stood together at the window of the hut and looked down over the flooded valley.

'All unhappiness is past now, my love,

see the sky is clearer,' Bassett said, 'the storms are over and we can start anew.'

And as he bent to kiss me, I knew he referred not only to the life which the villagers must build for themselves again, but also to our own two lives, our marriage and our love.

The publishers hope that this book has given you enjoyable reading. Large Print Books are especially designed to be as easy to see and hold as possible. If you wish a complete list of our books, please ask at your local library or write directly to: Magna Large Print Books, Long Preston, North Yorkshire, BD23 4ND, England.

This Large Print Book for the Partially sighted, who cannot read normal print, is published under the auspices of

THE ULVERSCROFT FOUNDATION